Colin R. Parsons is an author of children's and YA fiction, but his books are always enjoyed by a wider audience. He lives in South Wales with his wife Janice and two sons, Kristoffer and Ryan. He has been writing for many years and has a steady stream of readers. He writes in many genres including sci-fi, fantasy, steampunk and the supernatural.

Parsons's books are always exciting and filled with fast-paced adventure, peppered with intrigue and danger.

To find out more visit his website: www.colinrparsons.com

HOUSE OF DARKE

To Irchester Primary School.

Enjoy the book.

Colin R. Parsons

HOUSE OF DARKE

Pegasus

PEGASUS PAPERBACK

© Copyright 2015
Colin R. Parsons

A CIP catalogue record for this title is
available from the British Library

ISBN: 9781903490877

*This is a work of fiction. Names, characters, businesses, places, events and incidents are
either the products of the author's imagination or used in a fictitious manner. Any
resemblance to actual persons, living or dead, or actual events is purely coincidental.*

*Pegasus is an imprint of
Pegasus Elliot Mackenzie Publishers Ltd.*
www.pegasuspublishers.com

First Published in 2015

**Pegasus
Sheraton House Castle Park
Cambridge CB3 0AX England**

Printed & Bound in Great Britain

To Jan, for her unrelenting support and belief in my achievements.

Acknowledgements

I would like to thank all the readers of my work. It is definitely them that have kept me going through the years. Also the many friends and family who have always told me to keep going, even when I didn't feel I could.

Chapter 1

Bike trip

It seemed like a nice ordinary day for a bike ride – sunny, warm, and a million miles from school lessons. The serene countryside felt safe, and the trip was enjoyable. But unbeknown to the travellers a terrible evil was lurking and it lay in readiness for its victims to appear. She sensed its presence first – a feeling, a dull ache in the pit of her stomach. Its gloom and arrogance gave out the warning, but by then of course, it was already too late...

*

'I've got to pull in,' Pip urged again, his face creased up in agony. 'Come on, Zade, I need to pee.'

Zade looked behind at the ailing Pip and then to his sister, Meadow, and frowned. She knew he hated stopping on journeys but she needed to pee too and, so did Tina, Zade's girlfriend, by the look of her. She was nervously biting her bottom lip, too afraid to say anything; Meadow hated that about her. A girl is meant to speak up and say what she feels, she always told Tina.

They had been travelling for a couple of hours and, although he didn't want to admit it, Zade wanted to go too. But his stubbiness kept him going and the others were grumbling in his wake. They were all on bicycles, riding through the beautiful countryside on a day out. The pressures of starting back to school were way in the back of their minds.

'But where, Pip? I can't see any toilets. Can you? I just can't squat in the middle of nowhere,' Meadow moaned, glaring at her boyfriend.

'Sure you can. What do you think they did in the old days?' he said, still grimacing with the pain in his bladder. Tina said nothing, but a knot tightened in her stomach at the thought of dropping her three quarter jeans in the open. She'd never roughed it before and didn't want to start now.

'Zade, come on, man, let's pull over. Look, it will only take us five minutes and we can all relax. And we've still got plenty of time to enjoy the rest of the day. Five minutes isn't going to make much difference.' Pip gave the ultimatum.

It did seem a fair request, Zade supposed. He mulled it over and reluctantly agreed after seeing his girlfriend's tormented face.

They all left the empty main road and continued down a long lane. It was hot and they'd all built up a sweat. There was nowhere to relieve themselves here, the countryside was too open. They'd have to search until they found a clump of trees or bushes or something to hide behind. They eventually found what they were looking for, a deserted picnic area.

It was mid-September so the place was empty, but the weather taking a turn for the good meant that somebody would eventually drop by to picnic.

'Come on, before someone comes and catches us,' Pip teased. 'The last one to the bush is a banana.' His voice echoed as he dumped his bike with a clatter and sprinted away. He quickly disappeared into the dense woodland that engulfed the surrounding area.

Zade sat shaking his head. 'What a tool,' he mumbled under his breath.

'Don't worry, Teen,' Meadow said with a smile, 'you'll soon get used to Pip but you need to lighten up. If you wanted to go to the toilet too you should've said. Don't let my big brother bully you, or he will believe me.'

'I don't, honestly,' Tina replied sharply with a weak smile. 'It's just that, oh I don't know.' The answer she was going to give eluded her.

'What on earth do you see in him, Med?' Zade badgered her about her boyfriend for the umpteenth time.

'Oh, don't start on that again, Zade.' Meadow closed her eyes in a grimace and quickly dismissed it. 'I need to go right now too so I won't be long,' she said, cutting off the conversation – and with that she was darting off towards her boyfriend. 'Look after the bikes,' she shouted, panting as she ran. Tina looked innocently at Zade and puffed out a long breath.

'I don't bully you, do I?' he asked waiting for a positive reply, but not getting one.

'You can be a bit.' She paused, before adding, 'Hmm, overbearing sometimes, but I wouldn't let you bully me anyway,' she answered with conviction. Then she stopped, feeling the increasing pain in her bladder. 'I can't hang on much longer, Zade. But, saying that, I don't want that idiot to walk by as I'm doing it either.' She gave him a worried look and he responded with a beaming grin.

'He won't, I'll make sure of it. Let me go first and then I'll come back for you and I can guard you. I'll only be a couple of minutes, promise.'

Tina stood by the bikes on her own; it was quiet, but a weird feeling of dread came over her. A sinister vibe made her shudder but she couldn't make out why she felt it. *It was a nice place in the countryside, for goodness sake*, she told herself. *What am I fretting about?* she thought. Then Zade's voice broke her train of thought.

'Come on, there's a place over there,' he said, pointing to a clump of bushes that would keep her well hidden. They made their way up a gentle gradient. 'I'll stand here and I won't let anyone past; if they try to I'll kill them with one of my stares,' he again grinned. She liked the protectiveness about him; it was one of the qualities that drew her to him in the first place, besides his beaming smile. He was quite lean too, and fit. He loved playing rugby and his blond hair complemented his dreamy hazel eyes.

'What about the bikes?' she asked, breaking away from the moment.

'Don't worry about them, there's no one about. Who would want to pinch bikes in the middle of nowhere?' he said. 'Anyway, I can see them from here. Don't pee long.' Zade laughed at the terrible joke he'd just made. Tina shook her head in disbelief.

A white mist slowly drizzled its way in from the coast and descended on the woodland, almost unseen at first. It then thickened and the afternoon sun was soon devoured by its density.

'I can't explain it, but I don't like it here, Zade. There's something not quite right about this place,' Tina said in mid flow, keeping the conversation going so she could mask her embarrassment. She could hear him shuffling about on the grassy slope.

'This place is beautiful, just like you, Teen,' he said while facing away from her. When she had finished they made their way back down the gradient to the bikes. They heard the familiar echoed screams of laughter coming from deep within the trees.

'Listen to them? They're like six-year-olds,' Zade complained, trying not to – but sounding like – his parents.

'Can we get away from here? I'm freezing,' Tina announced, suddenly having to rub her arms. 'Where did this mist come from so quickly?' She was only wearing a short-sleeved T-shirt, a pair of three-quarter jeans and trainers. Seemed like a good idea when they left. It was hot earlier and the thought of a heavy jacket on a bike trip felt stupid at the time. But now she felt stupid anyway, looking at the goose-bumps on her arms and trembling violently. In fact they were all in similar clothing. But the only sensible thing any of them did was to carry a bottle of water.

'Yeah, wow, that did come in quickly, didn't it? I'll be back in a minute,' Zade said. 'I'm just going to find these two idiots first and then we can go. Don't worry, Teen; we'll be back on the road soon,' he said cheerily before disappearing

'D-don't be long, please, Zade, I don't like this place. There is definitely something – oh, I don't know – just don't be long.' She couldn't find the words to describe the fearful way she was feeling.

'Meadow, Pip – come on, you two, this fog is getting thicker. Where the hell are you?' he shouted in desperation. He eventually found them and they all made their way back. Tina was stood waiting not quite knowing what to do; she felt a little safer when she heard them returning through the woods.

'What are we going do, Zade? We can't ride in this,' Tina said. 'This fog is far too heavy to find our way back to the road.' She peered around, looking pretty scared. The light mist had turned into a thick soup and had cut visibility to almost two metres.

'Wow,' Meadow gushed. 'This is mental. What *are* we going to do, brother of mine? It wasn't this thick a couple of minutes ago. You're the man with the plan.' She looked directly at him and tilted her head.

'I don't know,' he snapped. 'I knew we should have kept to the stupid road.'

'We *had* to go to the toilet, Zade,' Pip said in defence. 'This fog would have come down if we were on the road or not,' he continued firmly as they stared each other out.

'Yeah, we did need to stop,' Tina added, nodding innocently. 'It's pointless arguing about this now. Let's just decide what we are going to do, and quickly. It's getting thicker and colder.'

'OK, I'm sorry, girls, I shouldn't take it out on you or Pip. I haven't got the answers, I didn't expect this either. This was just supposed to be a nice easy ride and a dinner in McDonald's somewhere or a cafe if we found one.'

'Zade, didn't you know where you were going when you said to go for this ride? I thought you'd done this route before,' Meadow scolded. 'What are we going to do now then?'

Zade looked sheepish and said nothing for a moment. 'I just picked a road and thought we could have a nice day out, that's all.' He shrugged his shoulders. 'I didn't know this was going to happen, did I? All right, I'll check the sat nav on my phone,' he said with confidence, 'I've only got to tap in the post code for home and it will take us back out,' he added with certainty. 'We can slowly push our bikes to the main road without riding them. When we're there, we can follow the pavement. Does that sound good?' It even sounded sensible to him.

'Sounds like a plan,' Pip chirped in, not normally agreeing with his girlfriend's brother. Zade checked his phone and sucked in air nervously. He then angrily puffed out his cheeks. 'I can't get a bloody signal,' he cursed, 'anybody else got a signal?' he said through clenched teeth. Everyone produced a mobile from their pockets.

'No, nothing,' his sister answered disappointedly. 'This is getting scary.' She was shivering now too and rubbing her left arm while looking at the screen.

'Me neither,' Pip said, shaking his head and looking into his palm. 'This is hopeless,' he mumbled under his breath, wishing he hadn't come at all.

'I haven't either, Zade, sorry,' Tina apologised still trembling. 'That makes all of us then? Four phones and not one any good.'

'It must be this fog that's causing the weakness of signal,' said Zade. 'Well, I'll have to find a house or garage or something, so they can help us out. This is stupid, all this modern tech and we're helpless.' Zade loved his gadgets, but this set him back. He was scrambling in his mind for an emergency idea.

'Where you gonna go, Zade? There's nothing here. We're in the middle of nowhere and we can hardly see our hands in front of our faces, never mind walking out to the road,' Meadow blasted. 'I can't even remember the direction we came in,' she said bluntly. Suddenly everyone realised their dire predicament: a simple bike ride had turned to disaster. Zade instantly made a decision.

'Look, I got us into this mess, I'll get us out.' Zade frowned. 'I'll go and find someone and tell them where you are. Just wait here with the bikes, I'll try not to be long.'

Tina looked at him blankly. 'No way, Zade, you're not going anywhere on your own; I'm coming with you.' What she really meant was: *you're not leaving me here with these two.*

'We're coming too,' Meadow announced speaking up for Pip, who was happy to sit and wait. 'I'm not leaving you wander around on your own. You could fall and there would be no one to help you. What kind of sister would that make me?'

'All right, all right, we'll all go; it would be better than you lot standing around freezing here I suppose, anyway,' Zade said reluctantly, before looking at his sister and forcing a grin.

'What are we going to do about the bikes?' Pip cut in, folding his arms. 'Mine is worth a mint and my parents would kill me if I lost it. I'm not leaving it here,' he said stubbornly, eyes fixed in a stare.

'Well, we can't take them with us, can we?' Zade snapped, eyes popping out of his head. He was getting more annoyed with Pip by the second. 'What do you suggest?'

'We're all in the same boat, Pip.' Meadow screwed her face up in anger, with him for once. 'Our bikes are worth a lot too,' she said angrily, shaking her head and sucking air through her teeth.

'Look, we'll leave them here and come back for them later,' Zade responded sensibly. 'We can't go pushing them through this,' he said pointing up into the grey abyss that engulfed them. 'There could be ditches or places where we can't take bikes and, they'll slow us down, won't they? We'll hide them over there.' He pushed his bike to a gap under a blackberry bush. 'No one will think of looking here – why would they?' Then he remembered he had a small torch in his saddlebag and a spark of comfort warmed him. He found it and switched it on. He grinned to himself. It didn't come on at first but he knew that if he smacked it a couple of times it would start working. A white beam of light flickered into life and he blew a breath of relief. 'OK, we have light, that's something.'

'Clever boy, where too now then, bruv?' Meadow asked again expectantly. She'd always relied on him when they'd been in trouble in the past and he felt like her hero.

'First things first – Pip, you hold Meadow's hand, so that the both of you are safe. I'll do the same with Tina, that way we can all be linked and no one will get lost. Stay close,' he said, a small plan evolving in his mind. 'Be careful, everyone, there could be all sorts of dangers.'

'I'm not leaving my bike,' Pip said standing defiantly. These words were like a slap in the face to Zade and he was about to go berserk, but he held back. He took a couple of breaths.

'Do you care more about your stupid bike than the safety of my sister?' he said slowly, steadily raising his voice to a higher, more aggressive tone. He stepped forward and stared deep into Pip's eyes. The cold air from his mouth vaporised into Pip's face. There was a pause and Pip, seeing that Zade meant business, backed down. Zade breathed rapidly and puffed out his chest. He knew Pip would relent.

'OK, OK, I'll leave the bike.' He could feel the colour draining from his face. He gave in, realising the awkward position he'd put himself.

'Now as I've said, if we all hold hands, I'll lead with the torch and we'll come back for the bikes later.' He was scared really but, being the oldest there, he had to take command. The other three were fourteen and he was fifteen, it wasn't much older, but all the pressure seemed to be on his shoulders. Pip didn't seem to want to take control and Zade worried for his sister's safety if things got tough. Would Pip crack under pressure? Easily, he thought. In essence he had two people to worry about, his own girlfriend and his sister. He hated to be in this position, but what could he do? He put that to one side and concentrated on the matter at hand.

It was really difficult to see which direction to go; the torch's beam didn't penetrate the fog and only reflected back. Until this fog lifts, this torch is going to be useless, he thought, but didn't tell the others. He felt foolish enough already without adding more problems to his day. The fog had drifted in from the sea. He knew that because there was a taste of salt in the air. The ground was soft and wet and so they began groping their way along. If someone lifted the mist and normality was restored they would all look ridiculous. It was hard going as they stumbled out of the picnic area. It felt like a bad disaster movie.

Zade came upon a long stick, which he could use as a staff, and picked it up. There were two elastic bands wrapped around the shaft of his torch that he'd put there ages ago to give more grip. He used these to fix the torch to the end of the branch. This way he could feel his way further with the stick and maybe see pitfalls with the beam.

'Wooo, very clever,' Tina cooed. Zade smiled to himself and walked on slowly, small compensation for his mistake. He still beat himself up over the position they were in, but what's done is done. The fog was a full blanket of grey and it wasn't possible to see more than a metre ahead now. Zade suddenly stopped and the others almost bumped into him.

'Are you OK?' Tina asked.

'What's the matter, bruv?' Meadow called as she gently tapped Tina on the back.

'There's a fence here, but it's been pulled down. There's enough of a gap that we can all get through,' he said, gently examining the barbed wire. He went to step forward and almost slipped before deciding to pull back.

'Whoa, don't move, you lot,' Zade said. 'There's a drop here too, to your right. Can't see or feel the bottom.' He felt with his stick and it slid into nowhere. 'You can all get through in single file, but take your time. I'll stand by the edge so no one falls over. Once you're all through the fence, just wait together and don't move any further in any direction. Watch your hands and arms so that you don't cut yourselves on the barbed wire too,' he instructed, sounding like one of the assistants in a theme park ride. They did as they were asked and Zade followed behind, but the damp earth gave way and he slid.

'Aaargh!' he cried and Pip spun around and caught his arm as he almost disappeared into the mist.

'Quick, help me,' Pip shouted in desperation. The girls quickly stepped back over and grasped his arm and collar.

'Pull him up. Come on, girls, pull.' Pip strained as he grappled with the leader. He was no lightweight, but with the combination of all their efforts they managed to drag him back. He lay back panting on the path, the soft cold mud soaking through his blue cotton T-shirt and jeans.

'That was too close. See what I mean, Zade, about you going off on your own?' Meadow scolded.

'All right, all right,' he repeated. 'I feel stupid enough without you going on, sis,' he snarled, embarrassed at the incident. He got back up and composed himself. 'Right, on the positive side, if there is such a thing,' he said sliding past each one to get to the lead again, 'if there's a fence there must be a farm or something – anything. It won't be long now, girls. We can get help and when the mist has gone. We can go back for the bikes and get home. How does that sound?' he said confidently. A warm feeling filled each of them – except for Zade – as his backside and lower back were damp and uncomfortable with the slowly caking mud. They resumed their positions and still consumed by the thick wall of mist they forged on. It was hard going, dips and bumps, slips and saves. The fog was a force and their limbs glistened with its gentle but unwelcome touch.

Come on there must be something close by, Zade thought.

Chapter 2

Darke House

They'd been slowly edging through the woodland for an hour or so when Zade raised his right hand and called a halt. He was lucky that he shouted or the whole party would have knocked him over; it was still pretty thick out there. When they'd passed through the fence earlier they all thought that help would be close at hand, but not so. Zade stood quietly and the others took a breath.

'This is hopeless,' he admitted. 'Where are we?' He let his emotions stray, which wasn't good for morale.

'I'm tired, I'm cold and I'm hungry,' Meadow complained, stamping her feet into the ground like a two-year-old as plumes of cold air belched from her mouth.

'I know, Meadow, so is everyone else, but you don't hear Tina and Pip complaining, do you?' Zade was well used to her tantrums.

'I'm pretty tired too – and hungry – and cold – if I'm honest,' Pip spoke up as Zade closed his eyes and rubbed his forehead in frustration. He thought Pip would just man-up a little, but obviously not. Tina smiled encouragingly and blew on her numb hands.

'OK, I know, I get it – we are all tired and the rest, but we also have to find somewhere before it gets dark. This fog hasn't lifted at all,' Zade said as he tried to make out the landscape, squinting into the distance but, the swirling and claustrophobic mist was too overwhelming.

'Zade, I'm scared,' Tina finally spoke up. 'This is a real problem. We're God-knows-where and I still can't get a signal on my phone. We could be walking away from help as far as we know,' she concluded.

'I know, Teen, but I'm telling you we'll find somewhere soon, I promise,' Zade responded unconvincingly and gave her hand a reassuring squeeze. 'I'm trying my best here,' he whispered in her ear. The sharp, cold air made her shudder and giggle. He smiled.

'Yeah, I'm still starving,' Pip grumbled again.

'You're not helping, Pip; we're all hungry, you know,' Zade replied with distaste. 'Come on a little further, there must be something nearby, surely,' he said, trying to convince himself more than anything. 'Something has to come good for us at some stage.'

He looked at them for support but they were too cold to drum up any kind of enthusiasm.

But things began to change. To his and everyone else's amazement, the fog suddenly became thinner.

'Yes!' he expressed, retrieving the torch from the end of his staff and snapping off the bands. He raised the beam and, because the fog was receding, the light stretched further, giving him more scope. Zade panned an area ahead in a sweeping motion. There were only some wisps of grey that reflected but as he continued he stopped and then retraced his line. He became filled with relief. He closed his eyes and a smile replaced the gloom.

'What are you doing, Zade?' Tina asked, curiosity taking her thoughts from the cold.

'Yeah, what's happening?' Meadow groaned from behind.

'There – look, I told you I'd get us all out of here, didn't I?' he said with a huge portion of confidence. Everyone squinted through the ever-moving shapes of mist and, saw, encircled by a faint black outline, a fantastic yellow glow. The shape in its humongous form looked like a building of sorts!

'What is that?' Pip asked dimly, as if expecting an answer. 'Can anyone make out what it is?'

'I'm hoping it's a house or hotel or something that can help us out, you idiot,' Zade grinned. *Is this guy for real?* he thought. He'd only known him for a couple of days and he had his doubts as to whether his sister would be better off with someone else. She was pretty, smart, and independent – a catch for any guy except Pip. He was just stupid and self-centred! It made him angry, but what could he do? It was her choice.

'It's not too far away by the looks of it, and the fog is definitely easing.' A real excitement tugged at Zade's stomach. He hated being wrong and this was a step in the right direction to pull their confidence back.

'If the fog is lifting why don't we just go back and get the bikes?' Pip looked at Zade.

'I'm freezing, Pip; the bikes can wait until we get warmed up, for God's sake. What is it with you and that stupid bike?'

Meadow was beginning to regret her relationship. Did he care more for that bike than her?

'Yeah, the girls are freezing, Pip. Why don't you think about someone else for a change?' Zade snapped. 'You are really beginning to get on my nerves.'

'All right – all right, I was only saying,' Pip mumbled.

'You and your bloody bike,' Meadow repeated. Zade turned away and grinned.

'S—sorry, Med, I didn't mean to.' He quit while he was behind.

'Let's go, we've got somewhere to head now, thank God,' Zade said, leading the way.

They walked from the damp soft grass carpet of the woodland onto more rugged ground. They were now standing on a coarse surface, a rough road of loose stone rather than the usual tarmac. The solid yellow glow of light, segmented the closer they got, revealed windows. 'Phew, it's definitely a house – well, bigger than that. It must be a country mansion,' Zade gushed as he craned his neck to take in the full enormity of it. 'It'll be warm inside too, Teen; a roaring fire I'd expect.'

She forced a smile through gritted teeth but was so cold she couldn't answer. As they approached the grounds to the front of the house there stood a sign on a big wooden frame. The plaque was suspended by two small chains that linked it to the main post. Zade pointed the torch at it and read:

'Darke House, woooow,' he said wiggling his fingers in a ghostly fashion. 'Wow, that's scary. It must be for the tourists,' he joked.

'Why is "Darke" spelt with an "e" on the end? They've written it wrong,' said Meadow, a little confused.

'Probably the name of the owner who built it,' Pip spoke up from behind. Everyone turned to face him and he looked at them. 'You know, his name must be Darke rather than, like, Dark of Night or whatever, you know?'

Meadow looked at him in amazement.

'Whoa, brainy,' she laughed. Her smile warmed him. He was full of himself by now and just peered back at her and mouthed the word, "sorry", to apologise for earlier.

Beyond the sign, though, the gigantic building engulfed the backdrop.

'It must be sixteenth or eighteenth century, I suppose.' Zade had no idea but tried to sound as if he did. Tina stifled a smirk and Zade looked at her with embarrassment. 'Well it could be.'

'I have no idea either,' she said. Zade looked at Meadow, knowing full well her history results were as bad as his had been.

'Eighteenth century I think, you can tell by the turrets.' Everyone looked again at Pip with quizzical expressions.

'How on earth do you know that?' Zade was astonished and his eyes widened. 'Are you some kind of swot?' he asked scornfully, itching to belt him at some point.

'No, not really. There was a building just like this on *The Antiques Road Show* the other day,' he said flippantly with a tinge of authority in his tone. 'I'm just observant.'

Maybe he's not that stupid after all, Zade thought. *Git*, he added. Before they could move any closer there came three bell chimes. They clanged through the mist like gunfire and hurt their ears.

'Aaargh, that's loud.' Pip held his ears while the pain made his face crease up. 'There must be a clock tower!' he shouted.

'No – do you think?' Zade shouted back. This guy was really stupid.

'Oh, my ears,' Tina cowered. 'I can't stick this.'

'Ooow, mine too! Make it stop, someone. Make it stop.' Meadow was crouched down and had her eyes shut and her hands cupped over her ears. 'Someone shut it off,' she demanded.

'It won't last long, I'm sure of it,' Pip said, trying to comfort her by putting his hands over hers.

'Let's get inside!' Zade shouted through the din. The others followed reluctantly, still trying to shut out the excruciating sound. The gravel crunched underfoot and made running impossible. Even walking was difficult. Then to everyone's relief, as suddenly as it started, the bell ceased.

'Jeeesus! Thank God for that!' Meadow was shouting when she now didn't need to. She realised what she was doing. 'I can still hear it.'

'My head,' Tina groaned.

'Likewise,' Pip added.

'It's only a bell; the ringing will stop soon. You lot are big wusses,' Zade laughed.

'Shut up, Zade. Feel free to ignore my brother, everyone, he always has to be the big guy.' Meadow glared at him. Zade tilted his head at an angle and gave her a look of contempt. Their hearing finally began to return just as Zade said it would.

'This ground is hard going,' Tina said to Meadow.

'Yeah, not what I was expecting to be walking on today, that's for sure,' she replied. 'Especially not in these flats.'

Tina grinned at the girlie comment.

They eventually arrived at the entrance. It was a typical country house: the gravel driveway stopped against an ascending stone staircase. There were two pillars at the bottom with plant holders crafted into the stonework. Bursting over the brim were beautiful yellow, red, and blue flowers to welcome guests. At the top of the steps there stood a huge wooden door. They all paused and looked on in anticipation.

'Come on.' Pip flicked his head in that direction. 'We're here now,' he said, finally accepting it. They reluctantly climbed their way to the top. The door itself was large and overbearing. Zade looked for a bell but there wasn't one, only a large twisted metal ring for a knocker. This was set at the centre and there was a knob halfway down to their left. Zade reached out and pulled the ring back and twice let it slam against its metal resting plate. The sound of metal on metal seemed to explode and echo through the house for an age. Tina hissed, hoping that they wouldn't have to deal with whatever was inside. They waited and waited but there was no response.

'Come on, let's—' But before Tina could say any more Zade repeated the action, drowning out her voice. But to her relief the same result ensued – nothing! The impending pause seemed to blot out every other sound around them.

'Oh my God, what are we going to do now? We'll have to go back and get the bikes,' she said, hoping they would all agree. She was shaking, but it was from fear more than anything else.

Zade put his arm around her. 'We can't go back now – it's too far and the mist is starting to thicken again, look.' He pointed behind them and it was swirling again. He felt bad enough already and angry with himself. He'd brought them all here and now there was no one in the house; after all they'd been through to get here. 'There must be someone inside. Why would the lights be on otherwise?' he probed. His anger consumed him, he felt like a volcano ready to explode. Filled with a burning guilt, he grabbed hold of the door knob and twisted with far more force than needed. It loosened! To his complete and utter surprise the door creaked open and he let go and stood back a step! A knot tightened in Tina's stomach – too late now. Zade stood with a gaping mouth and a quiet relief. He peered from left to right, waiting for someone to ask him to walk in but no one did. The door was open, he told himself, that's like an invitation. It was like stalemate on a chess board. Should they go in?

Chapter 3

Lord Darke

Zade felt that he was the one who should use his initiative and take the lead. So, he tentatively edged forward, totally feeling everyone's eyes on his back, and began to enter the property.

'Zade, no! We can't go inside,' Meadow hissed. 'It—it's private property; you know it's breaking and entering.'

'No, we can't, Zade. Meadow's right,' Tina agreed. 'It's against the law and, to be honest, I'm not going to be part of that,' she said, shivering and taking a step back.

'Well, I'm freezing and it looks warmer in there,' Pip said, stepping around all of them. 'I'm going in.'

They were all taken by surprise as he disappeared into the yellow glow of the foyer.

'Pip—Pip, get out of there,' Meadow demanded, trying not to shout but not quite managing it. 'You idiot, get back here.'

'Meadow, why are you trying to whisper? If no one heard that door knocker then I'm pretty sure they won't have heard us,' Zade explained, rubbing his hands.

'Let's go inside, it is freezing out here and, if the door is open anyway, then perhaps the owners want people to go inside,' Zade said, shrugging his shoulders and raising his eyebrows. Meadow was in two minds and relented. They strolled inside, except Tina.

'We're not going to steal anything, just get warm; you're freezing too.' He reached out to her and said, 'You're shivering, come on.' It did look cosier and if only to get warmed up for a couple of minutes. It was totally out of character for her but the situation was dire, so she sighed and gave in.

Stepping into the house was a whole world of difference compared to the cold they'd endured in the past few hours. It was the equivalent of a huge blanket being wrapped around your body after a bath. But that was soon forgotten in the sheer wonder of the interior. The greeting area was immense; in fact everything was spacious as they flooded the foyer. Firstly, from the high ceiling hung exquisite sparkling chandeliers that gave a real insight as to how the gentry lived in years gone past; but that was only a taster, as everyone's gaze seemed to fix on the staircases. It was like something out of a scene from a Disney film. There were two long, sweeping handrails made of what appeared to be marble. They engulfed either side like two arms welcoming any visitors inside. The stairs themselves were wide, wide enough to take six people abreast. Standing erect at the bottom of the staircases was a white pillar set on each side too, as if guarding the house from enemies.

'Wow!' Meadow said, almost overbalancing, gushing at its enormity. Beside all that, there were clocks, lots of them; a couple of grandfather ones standing in different corners. There were also clock faces fixed to walls with pendulums.

They then realised the ticking. Looking at the splendour of the house at first they hadn't noticed, but now it was prominent and a little intimidating.

'The owners like clocks,' Pip said, standing in front of one particularly highly-polished clock. He scrutinised the dials and design, totally absorbed.

There were also lots and lots of doors, all so highly polished that they reflected anyone who peered at them. *I wouldn't like to polish them every day*, Tina pondered.

'Don't touch anything, Pip. We shouldn't even be in here,' Meadow reminded him. 'Once we've warmed up, let's go. There's something not right about this place,' she said. Whether it was because they were inside some ones property or, well she couldn't put her finger on it.

'I wonder if the owners can help us,' said Zade, before looking over to Tina. 'This huge estate must run into the picnic area, surely?' He walked over to one of the doors. 'Perhaps the people who live here are still about somewhere.' He was going to grasp the handle when Tina stopped him.

'Zade,' Tina said. 'We can't just look around someone's home without their permission. My God, they could get the police onto us.'

'Nonsense, of course you can,' a voice replied.

Everyone stopped what they were doing. The voice came from high upon the landing, and immediately the front door clicked shut. All eyes focused on the top of the stairs. There stood a man in his mid-thirties, slight build, and immaculately presented. He was dressed in a black tunic, white britches, and long knee-length black boots as if he'd just landed from the eighteenth century.

'Don't be alarmed,' he said with a charming smile melting Tina's and Meadow's hearts. 'I am Lord Epacseon Darke and this is my humble domain, Darke House. Is there something I can help you with?' His voice was smooth and melodic. He smiled and descended the stairs – glided more than anything.

'We—err—um,' Meadow couldn't get her words out. 'Need help – yeah we need help – the fog,' she eventually spat, tripping over her own tongue.

'S—sorry we barged into your home Lord, umm… Mr err… Darke,' Tina gushed, 'but…'

'We got lost, Lord Darke, and we've been stumbling around in the mist for ages,' Zade cut in and pondered the situation. He walked away from the door he was about to open and joined the others.

'You must be hungry and thirsty then?' Lord Darke said cheerfully. 'Come into my dining room and warm yourselves, there's a roaring fire and comfortable furniture.' He swept past them and led the way further into the great house.

They followed and watched him as he opened up a set of double doors to their right. He turned and beckoned them to enter.

'Please, join me,' he said.

'What a charmer,' Tina whispered to Meadow. She was enjoying the luxury and splendour of the moment. They walked through and were greeted by another humongous room. This time there was a long oak table – one that you would expect after seeing any period dramas on television. It was set at the centre of the room and a fine crackling open fire was nestled next to it, just as the owner had described. There were two leather armchairs and a full settee. Pip looked around and was amazed to see more clocks. 'This guy is besotted,' he mumbled. 'I like clocks, but not this much.'

The one thing that drew all eyes though was a portrait above the fireplace of Lord Darke in all his splendour. In fact it was oddly surreal as it was set on the stairs in exactly the same place as they'd just seen him standing. He was wearing the same magnificent clothes and basically it looked as though it had just been painted.

'Oh my God, that's weird.' Tina's eyes were on stalks, 'This place is – I can't put my finger on it – but not right.'

'Do you always wear eighteenth century clothing?' Zade asked, smartly, but was dug in the ribs by his girlfriend who also gave him a stern stare with squinted eyes.

Lord Darke spotted this and smiled. 'Well only for the tourists, it makes things look more authentic, don't you know.'

'Sorry, Lord Darke, my boyfriend can be a bit rude at times,' Tina said, glaring at him.

'That's fine, no need to apologise,' he replied in a velvety tone and a warm smile to match. 'Here we are then – this is my favourite room in the house.'

What surprised everyone the most when they entered the dining hall was that the table seemed empty, and now was filled with a banquet. They looked at one another in amazement.

'Was this table laid out like this when we came in?' Tina whispered to Zade.

'I'm… err… not sure to be honest,' he said, scratching his head. The colourful array and presentation of food was spectacular.

'How did he know… we were coming?' Meadow asked suspiciously. She looked at Zade and he looked back blankly. Things had definitely taken a turn into the strange.

'Come, warm yourselves before you eat.' Lord Darke breezed past everyone and waved his arm toward the furniture in front of the fire. All were seated and Lord Darke took pride of place in front of them. He looked so at home, he must do this all the time, they all thought. He handed each of them a crystal wine glass and poured an orange liquid from a decanter, also made of leaded crystal. The weight of the vessel pushed down heavily – it was the real thing. Tina knew this because her father entertained guests at her home and they had similar glasses set in a posh cabinet.

'We're not old enough to drink alcohol, Lord Darke,' Tina explained. 'Thank you, though.'

'I understand, but it's only ginger ale to warm you up. Honestly, I promise you. If you've been wandering around my grounds for hours on a damp misty day like this, then a sharp drink of ginger will soon warm you up. It won't harm, I wouldn't dream of giving it to you otherwise.' He was shaking his head innocently and seemed genuine. 'And you all look frozen; this will warm the cockles,' he grinned.

They all nodded in agreement, not having a clue what he meant.

'Excellent,' he said, placing the decanter back on a small table. There was something strange about this man Zade wasn't sure of. He was generous and kind and, above all, polite, but there was definitely something amiss. Something sinister in the way his eyes sparkled and the false grin on his chiselled jaw. Zade hated smugness, which was ironic. But they wouldn't be there for long. So, they may as well enjoy his hospitality while they waited for the mist to disappear.

Tina and Meadow eased back onto the comfortable sofa and let the tangy liquid flow into their stomachs like molten lava. It was dreamy – the settee was like a huge glove that pulled them in. The aching in their limbs eased and their tensed bodies relaxed. The flames of the fire licked the inside of the chimney breast and the orange-yellow glow almost invited them inside the grate. They were all mesmerised by its hypnotic flare. On the mantle above the fire was a spinning disc inside a glass dome. It spun around and around. This was bliss, but their sleepy state was broken when Lord Darke spoke again.

'You must be hungry,' Darke said from behind. 'There is food aplenty over here.'

They didn't even realise he'd stepped away from the fireplace, but there he was seated at the head of the table. They had to vigorously shake their heads to refocus. All of a sudden the thought of food and the aroma was delicious. Pip's stomach began to rumble.

'Oops, sorry,' he said quickly, his face already red from the liquid but his embarrassment adding a deeper touch of scarlet to his cheeks. They were all seated, Zade and Tina to Lord Darke's right and Pip and Meadow to his left.

'This is like something from *Downton Abbey*,' Tina gasped.

'Yeah, I know what you mean, Teen,' Meadow said as she also watched the drama.

'We have to be going soon,' said Zade. 'We have to get back to the picnic area.'

'Zade, don't be so rude,' Tina said, cutting him another stare. 'Lord Darke is entertaining us.'

'Oh, that's OK, I understand,' said Lord Darke, entering the conversaion. 'He's probably concerned about your bikes.'

'But, how did you know we had bikes?' Zade asked suspiciously, lowering his eyebrows. 'We didn't mention anything about bikes to you, Lord Darke.'

'Well, it's not difficult really. I mean this place is miles from anywhere. How else would you have got here? You're all too young to have a driving licence and the buses don't run very often these days.' He gave another one of his famous beaming smiles. There was a gasp and everyone except Zade giggled. He hated being beaten and this guy was truly sharper that the carving knife that was lying next to that chicken. *He knows too much and has too many answers*, Zade thought.

'Come on, no more talk, eat up,' Lord Darke insisted. 'There's plenty more here and I have fresh lemonade or tea – I've more ginger too if you'd like some?' He giggled. Zade was too hungry to banter any more and so filled up his plate with meat and fresh salad. He wouldn't be able to think straight until his belly was full, so he kept silent. There was a big plate of buttered French bread rolls so he grabbed a couple and put them on the edge of his plate. Lord Darke topped everyone's glass with lemonade and they all got on with the job of loading plates.

'It's not very often that I entertain guests, so I'd like to make a toast if I may.' Lord Darke gestured for everyone to raise their glasses. 'To my newfound friends,' he said, swallowing back his whisky while the others sipped their fruit drinks. 'Excellent,' he continued. 'Go on, get stuck in – and there's a strawberry and cream trifle for dessert.'

'Wow, this food is amazing, did you cook it?' Meadow asked, chomping on a chicken breast.

Tina closed her eyes for a second and winced. She didn't believe in talking while you eat. She stared at Meadow with disapproval.

'Meadow!' Tina hissed through gritted teeth. Lord Darke seemed to take it with a pinch of salt and laughed it off.

'No, it's prepared especially for me,' he replied.

Soon the room was filled with chatter and giggles and the clicking of knives and forks. It was the best day they'd all had in a while, like an unexpected birthday party.

After a while they were all feeling quite full and talked amongst themselves. But, the quietest one at the table soon spoke up.

'Where's Lord Darke?' Pip suddenly asked. 'I didn't see him leave, did any of you?' he said, peering at the others. There wasn't a response for a moment.

'He was there a moment ago,' Meadow finally said, confused. 'Perhaps he's popped to the loo,' she suggested with a snort.

'What's the joke?' Pip asked.

'Well, how on earth does he take a leak in all that uniform?' Meadow said. 'It must take him ages.' She burst out laughing and Zade grinned back at her.

'Trust you to think of something like that,' he said. 'He's strange though. I don't trust him one little bit.'

'Shhh! He might hear you,' said Tina. 'He's been really nice to us, so we can't be rude to him. Who else would have treated us this way after more or less breaking into their home?'

'I understand what you're saying Teen,' Zade said in his defence, 'but there is definitely something strange about him. I just don't know what it is. Anyway, when he comes back we have to go and get our bikes. He should know roughly where they are and the mist has probably lifted by now anyway.' Zade looked around the room, creased his forehead and squinted.

'What's the matter, Zade?' Meadow asked her brother.

'It's strange, but there aren't any windows in this room.'

'Now you're fishing for things to confirm he's weird, but he's just nice – accept it,' Tina said.

'Come to think of it, Zade, I couldn't see any windows in the foyer, even though we could plainly see them from outside,' Pip said, adding to Zade's suspicions.

Tina suddenly kept quiet.

'This gets weirder and weirder,' said Zade. 'Come on, let's say our goodbyes and leave, I've had enough. I've got a really bad feeling in the pit of my stomach, something isn't right.'

'Oh, but it's lovely and cosy in here,' Meadow moaned, 'Do we have to?'

'Nah, I'm with Zade on this one, Med. Let's go find our bikes and get home,' Pip said. Tina was also up on her feet.

'Where is he, though?' Tina persisted. 'We can't just go without saying thank you.'

Zade breathed a heavy sigh and then sucked in air.

'Lord Darke? Lord Darke? We have to go now, it's getting late,' Zade called out. 'Hello? Lord Darke?' They waited and waited, but he didn't appear.

'This is strange,' Pip said, shuffling around the room. 'Where is he? You don't leave guests on their own, do you?'

'Look, Zade, there's a pen and paper over there,' said Tina, the idea popping into her head. 'We'll have to leave him a note. That's not being rude, it's the only way we can let him know and not leave without saying goodbye.'

'I can't write a note with this,' Zade said, looking at the quill feather and inkpot. 'This place is a bit too eighteenth century,' he gasped.

'Let me.' Tina pushed past him and dipped the quill in the ink and scratched out a note that was beautifully written.

Sorry we had to leave, but we couldn't find you, and it was getting late. Thank you, Lord Darke, for all your generosity.

'You are full of surprises,' Zade said, looking lovingly at her. 'Let's go out the same door that we came in; we don't want to get lost in here too,' he laughed and she grinned back. 'Ready, you two,' he said looking at his sister and Pip. 'Let's go.'

Chapter 4

Endless Stairs

'This can't be right,' Zade said, scratching his head as he opened one of the double doors to reveal a staircase. It was wide, easily as wide as the ones he'd encountered in the foyer. He stood for a moment and tried to make sense of it all. His expression was curious, yet jaded.

'Where did that come from?' Pip said, standing next to Zade and looking on bewildered. He then leant forward and popped his head through.

'This is nuts,' Zade exclaimed and gave a short nervous giggle, the kind of nervous laugh that didn't mean anything.

'This isn't possible.' Pip was rambling; his mind doing ten to the dozen.

'It can't be the right door, surely? I mean there are loads of them in this house,' Meadow uttered. 'We must have opened the wrong one.' She raked her fingers through her short, black, hair and then tucked it neatly behind her ears, as if to assert herself. 'No, this can't be right,' she continued shaking her head.

'Zade's right, Meadow, I'm sure we came through this set of doors. I mean, there aren't any more double doors in this room, are there?' Tina asked and with that gave another little look around, just in case she was wrong.

'There are no other doors, double or single, so these have to be the right ones,' Zade explained. 'What's going on?' I knew there was something strange about that guy. I said didn't I?' He hoped his train of thought was wrong. He was still clutching the handle and wished he hadn't opened the damn thing; he didn't need any more problems, but it was too late now.

'Oh look, this is stupid. He couldn't have actually changed the shape of the building – not while we were eating could he? I mean, come on, what is he – magic or something? Is he some kind of wizard?' Meadow said, faceitiously. 'There has to be another explanation for this.'

Everyone paused for thought and reasoned any answer's they could think of.

'Wizard,' Zade repeated in a whisper and looked at his sister cynically.

'OK,' Pip said, breaking the silence, 'this is a dining room, right?' He was stating the obvious, but doing so in a Sherlock Holmes demeanour.

'Yes, Pip,' Zade retorted sarcastically, 'this is the dining room, so what?'

'And this is a grand country house from the eighteenth century, right?' Pip spoke with a bit more authority.

Zade just nodded, waiting for the punchline. He didn't have the energy to counter.

'Well where is the door leading to the kitchen, then? I mean the guests would have been led into the dining room, like we were, but the kitchen staff would have to come in from another direction, wouldn't they? They wouldn't come in the same way as the posh people, so there should be at least one other door.' He concluded his speech like a barrister finishing his opening statement. 'So where is it?'

'He's right, Zade, a house this size would have a couple of doors in the dining room,' said Tina. 'I'm really freaked out by this. We need to get out.' Her face creased with the weight of fear, 'I'm really getting scared.'

'OK, all right; I'm going to try something stupid but simple,' Zade announced. He closed the door and waited a couple of seconds. While still holding the handle he looked at the others expectantly, but no one disapproved of his experiment. He then opened it again and held his breath before letting out a sigh. There were the stairs, plain as day. 'I didn't think that would work, but in this house it was worth a try,' he said, looking at the three bewildered faces. 'OK, there is no other way out so we have to take this way.' Zade nodded toward the staircase. He moved quickly through the door and straight up. He dragged Tina with him and Pip grabbed Meadow and followed hot on his heels.

'Where are we going?' Tina called out breathlessly, 'It's dark... I can't se—' As she said it, it began to get lighter. Zade looked ahead and was bewildered by the sudden illumination of light too.

'Boy, this is weird,' he panted. 'I don't know where I'm going, Teen; just keep up and maybe we'll get out of here. It's got to lead somewhere.' He was dashing ahead. All four of them were scared, not knowing what lay ahead, but they carried on. The staircase was a white spiral, with a solid cylindrical centre column. The outside wall was black, like a solid bank of ink. The air around them was cold but they kept warm running. They each kept to the centre as it wound around and around.

'Keep up, everyone, come on,' Zade shouted over his shoulder, his voice echoing. Trying to keep up but not having time to concentrate, Tina tripped and fell against the column. Zade felt the sudden tug on his arm and had to let go.

Tina's squealing instantly caught Zade's attention. She hissed and rubbed both her arm and hand vigorously, her face creased with pain.

'Are you all right, Teen?' Zade stopped and dropped back down to pick her up. 'I'm really sorry,' he said reaching out his hand to her.

'I—I'm fine,' she said, nodding with a grimace, not feeling fine at all. 'I just caught myself on the wall,' she said. She'd grazed her hand slightly and there was a red mark on her arm. The small jewelled ring that her mum and dad had given her for her birthday had traced a grey diagonal line on the surface of the column. She grasped Zade's hand and quickly got back on her feet. Within seconds the others caught up.

'Are you sure you're all right?' Zade again asked with concern.

'Yeah, yeah, I'm fine,' she said breathlessly and a little embarrassed, trying to dismiss the whole thing.

'We have to keep going, Teen,' Zade reasserted, 'in case that lunatic catches up with us. If he can create this, there's no knowing what he's capable of.' She smiled as best as she could and rubbed the back of her hand, but it burned and made her wince a little.

'Man, let's go,' Pip chipped in, sounding like a seventies hippy. 'He's probably not going to like it when he finds out we're gone. Let's get as far away from him as possible.'

'Ready,' Zade said and began climbing the stairs again, slower now, so Tina could keep up. The fresh welt on her left hand was starting to redden more deeply. They continued on up, it was getting to the point where each one was getting dizzy.

'Pip, can you hear him following us?' Zade called back.

'No, I can't hear anything – only our footsteps,' he answered as they climbed higher and higher. Suddenly Meadow stopped dead. She jerked back on Pip's hand and he let go reluctantly.

'What are you doing? We haven't time to stop,' Pip said angrily, dropping down two steps to where she stood. 'Come on, Meadow, we're losing Zade and Tina,' he urged angrily.

'No we're not,' she said adamantly. She put her right hand on her forehead and her left on her hip. She closed her eyes as if in pain. 'I don't believe this,' she muttered.

'What are you talking about? They've gone on ahead and we are losing them.' Pip was getting really frustrated.

'Wait!' she snapped and then calmly said again, 'Just wait, will you?' a little softer.

'Wait? Wait for what?' he retorted. Then there were footsteps. Soon, Zade and Tina came scuttling around the bend to the rear and almost crashed into them.

'What the heck is going on?' Zade gasped as he sidestepped Pip, only just missing him. 'How come you two got ahead of us? That's nuts!'

'Because we've been literally going around in circles,' Meadow said, folding her arms.

'What are you talking about? That's not possible.' Zade was getting more confused by the second.

'Well how do you explain us being in front of you two then?' she shouted. Zade, Tina and Pip were totally gobsmacked.

'How did you know we were going in circles, Med?' Zade asked. *I should have picked that up*, he thought.

'Look at the wall,' Meadow said, pointing at the mark that Tina had made by her fall moments earlier. There was the scratch, plain as day.

'B—but that means…' Tina was almost crying. 'Oh, what does it all mean?' She was confused and questioned herself. 'I can't handle much more of this.'

Zade let out a big sigh. 'It means that the dining room is only just below us. Look, let's go back into the dining room, then me and Pip can take him on.'

Pip gave a look of shock.

'Pip we can do this,' Zade urged. 'We can rush him and when he's on the floor we'll find another way out.'

'This is nuts.' Meadow was again nervously running her fingers through her hair.

'OK, I'm with you,' Pip nodded, reasserting himself. 'As you said, we push him to the floor, the weight of the two of us on one person should be enough,' he calculated. 'We can then escape.' He didn't really think what rushing Lord Darke actually meant, but in his frustration agreed anyway. The two girls didn't say anything; there was too much to take in.

'Well, the door can only be a few metres away so let's find it and get out of this mental staircase,' Zade was totally ready to fight. They walked back down but ended up at the mark in the wall again. Everyone went quiet.

'Where is it?' Pip finally said to anyone who would answer. 'This is getting way out of hand.'

'It—it's not here, how can that be? Oh my God, how can that be?' Tina was freaking out.

'How can anything be, in this mad cowing place?' Zade cursed and slapped his palm against the wall. He suddenly turned and looked to the outer wall and paused. He stepped forward, walking the width of the step. When he got to the edge, he reached out.

'What are you doing?' Tina asked. Zade didn't answer; he was too busy concentrating. He tried to press against the black surface and splayed his fingers, but to his amazement there was nothing to touch. There was, however, cold air and a sense of being inside a void. He pulled back, his breathing more rapid.

'What is going on here?' He reached out again and shuffled his foot to the edge of the step; it dipped into the abyss. 'What are we standing on?' he said softly, almost a whisper.

The light from above was gradually getting brighter, but the outer wall of the staircase was still inky black.

'What are we standing on?' Zade repeated. 'Are we in mid-air?'

'Oh, don't say that, Zade; you know I don't like heights.' Meadow moved on to the next step, up to her brother. She slowly slid her foot to the outer edge and stopped when she couldn't feel anything. She quickly shuffled back toward the centre column where she felt the safety of a solid object.

'Oh my God—Oh my God.' She was frantic. Soon the light was strong enough to see above and then the reality of their situation came about in a mechanical volley of sounds that erupted. That was followed with a frightening vibration

Clunk... shhhhhhh

Clunk... shhhhhhh.

The steps and the pillar seemed to tremble with every overbearing attack.

'Oh my God, what is that?' Tina said, shaking violently. Pip was gobsmacked and tried to steady himself against the pillar.

'Jesus, look!' Zade pointed upwards and stared intently at what he'd found. Meadow, Tina, and Pip reluctantly looked in the same direction. It seemed like the sky was falling in slow precise movements, with thunder as its army. But not a smooth blue, summer sky by any means, a sky filled with sharp spear-like weapons descending with murderous purpose.

These rods were fixed into the ceiling and now chillingly, the teenagers realised, the ceiling was descending!

Clunk... shhhhhhh.

Clunk...shhhhhhh.

'God, those spikes will be on us in minutes,' Zade croaked, his breath laboured.

'Can't we just jump off?' Pip asked, looking ominously towards the black wall.

'Jump off to where?' Meadow asked, recoiling darkly. 'I'm not jumping anywhere. I can't.'

'We're all gonna die,' Tina screeched.

'We're not, we're not,' Zade said, trying desperately to think of an off-the-cuff plan. 'There must be a way off this thing.'

The sound was getting louder and the vibration increased. It was like a theme park ride, but this one the customers wouldn't be going home after.

'Well if there is, we've got to find it fast because those spikes are getting nearer,' Pip said. He always seemed to come up with the wrong thing at the wrong time.

'That definitely isn't helping, Pip,' said Zade. 'Let's try and find something.' Zade gave him a look that could burn a hole in wood.

'Don't leave us,' Meadow shrieked.

'Where we gonna go, Med?' Zade shook his head. 'We're on a spiral lift that goes around and around.'

'I don't care, we all stick together,' she said firmly.

'There's no way out?'

'What if we stayed on the lowest part of the steps, then maybe the spikes won't reach us?' Tina suggested through her sobbing.

'Because that's why,' Zade said, pointing to the spikes that were now elongating as he spoke. 'They are going to reach us however low we go.'

'That's it then. We've come into this mad house to die on this stupid staircase!' Tina exploded. 'Why? What did we do wrong?'

'Tina, we can't give up. Get a grip,' Meadow boomed angrily. Tina looked back in complete astonishment. 'There's got to be a way off. Come on, think, guys.' They were within six metres of the deadly spikes but no one could come up with an escape plan. The floor shuddered with every mechanical clunk, almost knocking everyone off balance.

'What the hell do we do?' Pip screeched.

'I don't know. Why have I always got to have the answers?' Zade shouted back through the din of the mechanical doom machine.

'I don't want to die,' Meadow sobbed.

'Well neither do I!' Tina snapped back.

'This is mad,' Zade said as the pointed spears got closer and closer.

'What are we gonna do?' Tina screamed again, this time her eyes glassy and her bottom lip quivering.

'Come on, let's jump,' Pip said. 'We break a leg – we break a leg. Or die, we're going to die anyway aren't we?'

'Jump?' Tina cut in. 'I don't want to jump.'

'I—I can't j—ump,' Meadow trembled. 'I just can't. I'm too scared to jump.'

'Well, how do you want to die?' Pip said simply. 'An agonising death on the end of a skewer? Or a quick death with no pain?' Pip was being deliberately sarcastic. 'The choice is ours. I don't want to die either, but I'm not going to end up like a human kebab.' This brought a nervous smile from all of them and also put things in perspective.

'Med… he's right.' Zade put his arm around her shoulder in a brotherly hug. This always seemed to soothe her. 'There is no other way,' he whispered gently in her ear. She began to sob; great, bulbous tears rolled down her cheeks. She knew it was the only way. She didn't want it to be, but that was the way of it. The spikes were within three metres and the clunking was the most violent yet. The whole structure shook as if ready to collapse. There was no more time left to deliberate. She looked at the others.

'I'm ready,' she said simply. Tina had mulled it over too.

'I'm ready too,' she announced.

'We all jump then?'

No one answered – only nodded.

Zade pulled up to the end as the spikes descended upon them at an alarming rate. They reluctantly stood side by side, knowing time was short. The two boys stood on the outside and the girls between them. Their bodies were trembling, as they stood with their eyes closed. Zade was holding Tina's hand and she held Meadow's. Meadow gripped both Pip's and Tina's hand with force. Each one could hardly hear a thing. The continuous drum from above only added to the thump—thump—thump of their hearts bursting in their ears.

'When do we jump?' someone said. There was a collective pause that gave way to the grinding, mechanical sound of death. The fear was only balanced by the gut-wrenching nerves in their stomachs. Meadow could feel the tension through her grip on Tina's hand – sweaty and tight like a vice. No one seemed to be doing anything. The blades must be nearly to the point of spearing them by now. Was this going to be their fate? Each one pondered.

'Well?' Pip shrieked. His stomach heaved but he couldn't find it in himself to push forward.

'Come on, someone do something! I can feel the air moving above my head,' Tina screamed frantically.

'*Now!*' Zade shrieked, bursting over the edge and taking them all with him.

Chapter 5

Balcony

As they jumped, Meadow's grip on Tina's hand broke free, leaving the two pairs separated. Both Pip and Meadow landed almost immediately and had only fallen about a metre or so. They'd braced themselves, expecting to be flying through the air from a huge height. Instead, they hit the ground and snapped away from one another, both falling awkwardly and crumpling as they landed. Meadow screamed as she hit the ground and fell onto her back. Pip grimaced and clenched his teeth as he too sprawled on the floor. They lay there winded, trying to catch their breath. They were too scared at first to open their eyes.

'Has anyone opened their eyes yet?' Meadow finally asked, not wanting to open hers first.

'No, I was too scared,' Pip answered croakily. 'But hearing your voice has certainly made me feel better. Are you hurt?' he asked, immediately looking around.

'Aw, sweet. I'm fine,' Meadow said, taking a peak. 'Are you all right?'

'Yeah, I seem to be all right too,' he replied, checking various parts of his anatomy.

'Pip, where are they?' Meadow asked. She realised they were on their own and started panicking.

'I don't know, but where are we?' He was confused and tried to make sense of his surroundings. They were lying on a grand balcony.

Pip helped Meadow to her feet once he'd got up. They found themselves overlooking the greeting area; they were actually standing at the centre of the balcony and there were beautiful flowing marble staircases on each side.

'How on earth did we get here?' Pip said. 'We're back to the place where we came in.' Pip was slowly beginning to understand how things worked in here. 'This place is playing with our minds.'

'I don't care about any of this. I just want to know where my brother and Tina are,' Meadow expressed sharply. 'I just don't understand what's happening. I want to go home. I'm scared, Pip. I want to go home.'

'I know, but we have to find them first,' Pip said sensibly.

'I know,' she responded, glassy-eyed. 'I wouldn't even think of leaving without them. It's just, I hate this place.'

'They can't be far away and, once we've found them, we can get out. If it's any consolation, I'm as scared as you, Med. I don't understand any of this either and I don't like what I don't understand.'

'All right then, we find my brother and Tina and get out of this stupid place. We've only been separated for a couple of minutes,' Meadow surmised.

'Zade?! Tina!' they cried out. 'Zade, come on; where are you?' Both their voices echoed endlessly in the vast void of the mansion.

'This can't be real,' Pip reasoned. 'There are too many weird things happening.'

He walked over to the balustrade and touched the cool marble surface. 'If this isn't real it doesn't feel like a prop from a film. This marble is solid and cold,' he said as he jumped up and down on the spot.

'What are you doing?' Meadow said. She looked puzzled and a quirky smile banished the fear for a moment.

'I'm only trying to work out if any of this is fake. It doesn't seem to be. It's either we're cracking up or this is all real.' He stopped and rested both hands on the balustrade as if he was the Lord of the manor surveying his domain. 'Look, there's the door where we came in. It's only over there,' he said, pointing below. 'Let's go outside and find help. Maybe if we found a police station they could come here and search the place.'

'No way, Pip. I'm not leaving here without my brother and Tina,' she said in retaliation. 'We find them first and then we get out, no question.'

'Look, Med, what if they are already outside? Let's go out first and if we can't see them, then come back in.' He looked at her and raised his eyebrow slightly. He seemed genuine enough and she thought she knew him by now. But, was he trying to get out and save his own skin? She wasn't sure.

'OK, but if they're not there then I'm coming straight back in,' she said.

He nodded meekly in response. They glided down the staircase and jogged toward the entrance. Pip quickly gripped the door knob and twisted. The door clicked in reply and creaked open and they darted outside with a sense of relief.

But it wasn't what they expected when the door slammed shut behind them. They were most surprised to find that they weren't outside at all, but in another large open room.

Pip's heart sank.

It was a circular room, this time with a series of doors all identical in style and colour.

'Oh my God. I don't believe this place.' Meadow was flabbergasted. She felt sick and frustrated and didn't know what to do. 'We've only got ourselves into deeper trouble,' she said. 'We should've stayed where we were.'

'This is completely nuts, a bloody nightmare. We should be outside. How did this happen?'

A voice boomed overhead as if on cue and made them physically shudder.

'Choose carefully the door in which you enter, for there are dangers,' the sound of the voice echoed. 'One door in particular will help you find your friends, but which one? The choice is completely up to you.'

'Let us out of here, you maniac,' Pip screamed at the ceiling.

'Good grief, he knows where we are? All this time and he's been watching us,' Meadow cursed. 'I've been bloody scared out of my wits and he's playing us like a piano. Who are you and what do you want with us?' she shouted, looking above to see if there was a sign he was in the room. 'Where are you – you coward?'

'Please, just let us all go! Where are Zade and Tina?' Pip screamed. 'You can't keep us here.' Their ranting was futile.

'You're bloody mad!' Pip bellowed.

'No, ya think?' Meadow replied, rolling her eyes. 'We're stuck in a house that we can't get out of, Pip. Yeah, I would say he's mental.'

'All right, Med, don't take it out on me. I'm stuck here too, you know,' Pip snapped back. 'I'm only trying to figure him out.'

'OK, OK, I'm sorry, Pip; there's been too much going on. I'm worried, especially if the others are in danger. He said one door will help our friends, so what danger are they in?'

'It's a riddle. Everything this guy does is a riddle of some sort.' Pip was scratching his head. 'One thing though, Med, I do like a good riddle. Me and Jake, Robbo, and Dave do riddles all the time. We have a… a riddle club,' he said with a spark of excitement in his eyes.

She looked at him curiously. 'A riddle club? Oh my God, you're a nerd,' she said in realisation. 'I'm going out with a nerd.'

'I wouldn't go that far but, um, well, you know on Wednesdays? When I don't see you, that's where I am. We work out all sorts of problems,' he said excitedly, as if a confession was his release.

'Riddle Club? Anything else I should know? Ballroom dancing classes, perhaps?' Meadow said with a giggle.

He looked hurt.

'I'm only joking, you idiot. We all need a hobby, yours is just a bit different from other boys I know. Probably that's why I like you. Some are sporting, gorgeous, and hot, and I chose you.'

He looked back at her and a warm smile filled his face,

'But saying that, don't expect me to join. You're the nerd and that's enough in this relationship.'

'Right,' he said with a grin. He refocused and snapped back into riddle mode. 'One door is different,' he repeated as he walked around the room. The door they'd entered through originally was no longer there. There were no windows and only one single chandelier hanging from the centre of the fantastic sculptured ceiling. There were ten doors, all identical in size, colour, shape, and design.

'One different… one different… what if? Hmm… no, I don't think so.' He kept mumbling to himself as he examined each one. 'It could be… no.'

Meadow stood back and watched, with a blank expression.

'They're all the same, Pip,' said Meadow, breaking his concentration. 'He's playing us again, they're all exactly the same. Are you even listening to me?'

'Not all; he said one is different,' Pip growled. 'Meadow, you're going to have to give me quiet time. I can't concentrate when someone is distracting me.'

'Oh sorry, yeah, quiet time. How stupid of me,' she grumbled. Pip walked in a complete circle, examining each door in painstaking detail. He began muttering and shaking his head intermittently. He stepped back a couple of times and returned to a door. Then he continued and did the same again.

'They all have the same brass knob for a handle, inset, framework, colour, and size.' He talked mainly to himself and puffed out his cheeks in frustration. He went round again and again to each door. The more times he went the more frustrated he became and the more annoyed Meadow got too. Pip pulled at his hair and ground his teeth. He rubbed his chin and puffed.

'This is pointless. We should just try them one by one,' Meadow interrupted, her hands planted on her hips. 'This is doing my head in.'

'No!' Pip reacted. 'That's just what he wants us to do, can't you see?' He was ranting now like some mad professor. 'If we just barge forward then we could open a door that lets in a wild dog or a deadly gas or—or a mad axe man.' He was in full swing and breathing hard.

'All right, all right. I'm sorry. I just want to find my brother and his girlfriend – is that too much to ask?' Meadow looked at him as her eyes again began to well up.

'I'll find the answer; just let me think for a minute, please.' He gazed back. 'I will find the answer.' His look was stern.

There began a low rumble and the sound of stone rubbing against stone.

'What—what is that?' Pip looked from side to side, then up and down. The floor was vibrating, not violently, but gently. They looked at one another and steadied themselves.

'What's happening?' Meadow was freaking out.

'I don't know—' Pip stopped mid-sentence. 'It's the floor,' he said. 'It's opening, look!' He pointed at a crack.

At the centre of the circular room a hole was appearing, pulling away from itself. Pip walked up to it and looked in. It was a perfectly round hole about the size of a golf ball, but it was slowly getting larger as he watched.

'Curious,' he said with trepidation.

Within seconds it was about the size of a tennis ball.

'Good grief, we haven't much time. There is nothing but blackness down there,' he said with intrigue. 'Ingenious,' he commented in admiration.

'What, Pip? Don't praise this idiot, what do we do? He's trying to kill us.'

'I don't know. Think, boy, think,' he said to himself. He looked frantically at each door again but they still all looked the same. When he was with his mates, they had time to work things out, time to ponder. But he didn't have time now, only a rash move; he didn't do rash moves. A bead of sweat appeared on his brow. The hole was now the size of a football and getting bigger.

'Pip, do something!' Meadow screamed. 'It won't be long before it's completely open.'

Pip was at a loss as to what to do next. No answer would come into his head. The grinding continued and cool air wafted from the ever-increasing void. Pip moved quickly, examining everything again as he went around and around, exactly as he'd done on numerous occasions. His breathing became erratic and his lips felt like dry rubber. He was so engulfed in trying to solve the problem that he didn't see how big the hole was at that point. It was now half the size of the room and still growing.

'Pip, come on! Open a door – any door! Please come on or we're going to die.' Meadow followed him, tugging at his polo shirt. Tears streamed down her face, smearing her make up.

'I'm trying – I'm trying! Let go! I'm trying to think,' he screeched, pulling her hand away.

'Well try *harder!*' she bellowed. 'If I had a gun I'd blast these doors off their bloody hinges.' Pip stopped and stood bolt upright. It felt like he'd been hit by lightning, his eyes sparked with new purpose.

'Oh my God! That's it,' he shouted turning and cupping the back of her head. He gave Meadow a big, forced kiss that almost pushed her lips into her skull. He quickly turned back and scanned the doors in a sweeping motion, like a lighthouse beam searching for stricken ships. He searched each door again and a flicker of gratification made him grin. They were standing on a narrow strip of floor now, like a rim on a bicycle wheel, and it was edging its way to the wall.

'What, Pip? What is it? There's no time, you idiot!' she screeched. 'Don't think about it – just do it!'

'That's it, Med. Hinges – there aren't any on one door. Look,' he said. Sure enough, out of all the doors there, only one was without hinges. He'd been looking at the doors themselves, but in fact it was what held the doors up that he should have been looking for. The problem now was that they were directly opposite the door they needed to open and the floor was just wide enough to get around.

'Meadow, follow me quickly,' he screamed excitedly. They ran clockwise toward the door. The floor was retracting and there was now less than half a metre.

'We're not going to make it,' she panted from behind.

'Yes we are – yes we are,' Pip shouted confidently as they approached. He just hoped that the door itself would open easily and inwards. He came to a stop, his heels already hanging over the edge. Meadow sidled up beside him, rubbing her back as tightly as she could to the wall.

'Pip it's too lat—' she couldn't finish because Pip had grabbed her arm and they were now sliding at great speed down some kind of chute. They tried to speak but it was impossible. Down and down they spiralled out of control and any idea as to where they were headed was not forthcoming.

Don't let me die, please don't let me die, Meadow thought, the words rattling around in her head. Then they tumbled out of the chute and onto a platform.

Chapter 6

Clockwork

'Oh Jesus,' Zade hissed, vigorously rubbing his thigh; it burned. 'That bloody hurt,' he cursed. Then it hit him – he was alone. He stopped to take in his surroundings but it was too dark. The ache in his thigh disappeared momentarily. He and Tina were holding hands only moments earlier, but where was she now? Besides that, where were Meadow and Pip too? He began shouting for them. 'Teen, Meadow, Pip! You lot all right? Where are you?'

The silence engulfed his mind. He searched everywhere he could, groping on the ground like some sort of scavenger, but it was hopeless. The blackness was overwhelming. He just couldn't find anyone, he was too scared to think what danger they maybe in. Suddenly, light leaked into the room or wherever he was. The beam came from nowhere. There wasn't a strip light or bulb in sight yet it was getting easier to see, really strange. It was like dawn was breaking, but he wasn't outside, or at least he didn't think he was anyway.

'Tina, *where are you*?' he shouted again, a sick feeling grabbing at his stomach. And then he saw her; he couldn't speak. His girlfriend was slumped on the floor and not moving, not far from where he'd landed but it was dark then.

He couldn't believe she was laying there, only three metres or so away. He froze, then ran his fingers through his blond hair and rubbed the back of his head, a habit he'd always fallen into when things were out of his control. He came to his senses, quickly got to her and gently rolled her over onto her back. Was she breathing? He didn't know, so he put his ear as close to her mouth as he could and listened.

She was breathing, slow and shallow; he could hear and feel the soft warm puff on his cheek. She was also bleeding from a cut on her forehead so he took a closer look with the emerging light.

It was only a slight graze. 'Oh, thank God.' He heaved a sigh of relief. He didn't like the idea that her eyes were closed, it frightened him. He panicked. 'Tina—Tina! Speak to me. Please, speak to me?' he said as softly as he could and, gently shook her to bring her round. *Jesus, Jesus, I'm not supposed to move her am I? I don't think I am anyway*, he thought. *Health and safety, you're not supposed to move someone – the patient.*

He'd seen it on some soap on telly and realised it could harm the person if they were moved. *Oh, God, I hope I haven't harmed her.* Just then, though, Tina began to come around. Her eyes flickered open like freshly lit candles. She smacked her dry lips and ran her tongue through the slit. Zade's eyes burst out on stalks and his mouth fell open.

She felt slightly dizzy. 'Wha… happened?' her dry voice croaked.

'Stay still and take your time,' Zade said, trying to comfort her. 'You've had a fall.'

'What happened?' she repeated. 'Where are we?' Then it hit her. She remembered the jump and she clenched her eyes shut in frustration.

'Are you all right, Teen?' Zade was deeply concerned, 'I— I thought I'd lost you,' he admitted. There were tears welling in his eyes, a human side that he didn't bring out often.

'Help me up,' she asked, cutting into his confession. 'I'm fine.'

'You're not supposed to move after a fall,' he informed her.

'I really am fine, Zade, just get me up or shall I do it myself,' she insisted forcefully. He relented and reluctantly lifted her into a sitting position. She sat for a few seconds taking deep breaths.

'Is your back OK?' he said, trying to work out what to do for the best.

'I'm all right, really, don't fuss; fussing gets on my nerves,' she complained and took another breath to compose herself. She lay her forehead on her palm and felt the warm wet patch of blood. 'I'm bleeding,' she said. Her eyes widened when she saw the stain of red in her hand.

'It's not much, Teen,' he said. 'Only a graze, where you must have hit your head when you landed.' He tore a small piece of his T-shirt hem, so she could stem the trickle. She dabbed it a couple of times and it stopped almost straight away. But she kept looking at the material for a while after, just in case.

'Where are we now and where are Pip and Meadow?'

'I don't know, Teen; we're here and they're not,' he said, mystified, and looked around hopelessly. 'I know we all held hands but they must have broken away somehow. I mean, we only fell a really short distance so where could they have gone?'

'We've got to find them.' Tina was worried. 'I hope they're OK. They could be in serious trouble – hurt more badly than me.'

'I know, I'm just as worried as you are. Let's find our way out of here first. They can't be far.' Zade was looking around again as he helped Tina to her feet. She felt a little unstable at first but gradually found her balance. Her head throbbed above her right eye, but she could handle that.

'We were only just standing on a spiral staircase, how on earth did we get here? In fact, where is the staircase?' she asked, gazing at the ceiling. Zade didn't have any of the answers to give her.

'Well, we jumped and landed. I stayed conscious; you were only out a minute or so. But like you said, there's no trace of the staircase or anything else really, just this corridor,' he said with conviction. 'This place gets weirder and weirder. It's as if we're being played with. Darke must have control of this house and everything in it. I know, I know, that sounds impossible, Teen, but how else do you explain what's happening?'

'I know what you mean, it's like we're being watched, but how is that possible without CCTV. Let's go find your sister and Brainbox, and then work out a way to get out,' she said. 'Which way should we take?'

Zade looked from side to side.

'I don't know if it really matters, I really don't. It's a long corridor and there's only that way or that,' he said, pointing ahead and behind. 'Let's go this way then,' he concluded moving straight ahead. They strolled for a while without talking only taking in the surroundings. There wasn't really much to see besides the walls and ceiling, which were eggshell-coloured. There was, however, also the faint whiff of oil for some reason. Zade took a couple of sniffs.

'Can you smell that? I don't mind the smell itself, but why would we smell it here?'

'Yeah, it's like Dad's engine in his car. I can't work any of this out Zade, we're supposed to be in a house, not a garage,' she puzzled. The graze on her forehead was slowly reddening and a lump was forming.

'I know what you mean; it smells like a mechanic's dream.' This made him think of the oil he used on his bicycle chain. 'I wish I hadn't suggested that stupid bike ride in the first place. I mean if it wasn't for me you lot would be safe at home now.'

Tina grabbed his hand and squeezed it gently.

'Don't blame yourself. It was a great idea to go for a ride. No one expected that mist to come in like that. And no one expected things to turn out this mental either. I'm sure wherever Meadow and Pip are now, they're not blaming you.' Tina was trying her best to comfort him. 'Stop beating yourself up over this, will you?' She smiled at him with her soft blue eyes.

'I really hope they are OK, though.' He looked worried and concerned about Meadow more than Pip.

'Look, Zade, Meadow isn't stupid and Pip… well Pip will look after her.' Even Tina wasn't convinced of that.

'He'd better,' Zade said as he clenched a fist. Tina felt his frustration.

'Come on, let's find out where we are,' she said, pulling him forward, her voice echoing slightly in the long distance of the chamber.

They'd only been walking a couple of minutes when Tina stopped.

'That's weird.' She let go of Zade's hand and put her arms out as if balancing on a tightrope. Zade said nothing at first and just peered at her, his eyes squinting in confusion.

'Is your head aching again?' he asked.

'It's not my head. Can't you feel that – it's weird?' she repeated.

He looked at her again as if he thought she was losing the plot.

'Can I feel what? What's weird? What's with the arms?' Zade asked. 'Why are you trying to fly?' he chuckled. She looked deep into his eyes and gave a beaming smile.

'I'm not, you idiot. I—I don't know but, is this corridor slowly starting to slope?' she said, bringing her arms down to her hips.

'What do you mean, like a gradual slope – like a kid's slide?' Zade looked at her and sighed; things were already off the scale and he didn't need any more surprises.

'No, not like a gradual slope in the floor; I mean it's actually beginning to slope away from us as we are walking on it,' Tina said. She was serious. She also glanced from side to side, as if to check whether she was seeing things or if it really was happening in real time. There weren't any reference points in which she could prove her claim. Everything around her was one solid colour. There wasn't a pattern or line that would back up her statement.

'No, it can't be.' But even as Zade said it he gradually felt the floor lowering away from him too, dropping, sloping off. Whilst this descent was taking place there was also a kind of grinding noise emanating from the end of the corridor, like metal on metal. The smell of oil too was getting much more pungent.

'It is moving, Teen, I can feel it now, you're right.' He looked at her and his forehead creased in puzzlement.

'Zade, what is that noise? I don't like this,' she said, trembling.

'Uh… um… OK, let's turn around and head back,' he said simply and clasped her hand. 'If it's dropping one way, then we'll go the other way.' They began walking away from the noise and the grinding soon faded. But the way back was getting steeper, almost like the sloping of a corridor on a ship as it began sinking.

'Come on, run!' Zade sped off and pulled Tina along with him, but it was no use. They found that they were tilting their bodies forward to counter-balance the angle.

'Oh my God, Zade, I'm slipping,' Tina screeched. 'It's getting too steep.' Zade was also finding it difficult to move without slipping back so he gipped more tightly on her hand.

'How high can this thing go?' she growled.

'I don't know, just grab something – anything,' he shouted forcefully, desperately looking for something to hold onto himself.

'What—what do I grab?' Tina was well into panic mode, 'Zade, there's nothing to grip on to.'

Zade realised she was right and they were gradually falling back together, back towards the noise and the smell again. They tried to lean into the angle, but by now it was too great.

'No – no – no, get on the floor and crawl, quickly,' he hissed and so let go of her hand. 'If we crawl we can still move forward.'

Tina didn't answer – she was too busy trying to grope her way ahead. Crawling made it a little easier to grapple forward and they were making slow but sure progress. Centimetre by centimetre they edged on but the incline was at such an angle now that it felt more like climbing a wall rather than crawling along the ground.

'I—I can't hold on, Zade, help me,' Tina gasped, sliding away from him. Zade tried to grab her and, when he reached out, lost grip too.

'No!' he screamed as he slid past her. Tina squealed as she tumbled down behind him. The grinding sound of metal soon became more audible the closer they got to the source.

'Roll onto your back, Teen—Tina, roll onto your back.' She slid straight into the side of him and they righted themselves. Now they were sliding on their backs at the same rate so they linked hands again. Ahead, the sound revealed itself in the most horrific way. They looked on helplessly; the clunking and grinding actually were big metal cogs, set out in two lines, four each side. They were rolling into each other and perfectly synchronised. There was obviously a purpose to this and then they saw it immediately. To the right of them was a huge clock face. It was the biggest clock they had ever seen. Big Ben, the clock tower in London, came directly to their minds. It did look the same design as that huge landmark; it had a transparent face with large black numbers and three hands of different thicknesses: the hour, minute, and the second hand.

The second hand was ticking away in time – tick, tock, tick, tock – but the wheeled cogs were going at a much faster rate. They reminded Zade of his parents' old electric lawn mower when the blades were in full spin. He'd almost caught his hand in them when he was little and so the horror of that memory came flooding back. But this was far more dangerous and it wasn't just his fingers he was worried about. This machine was going to chomp on the two of them and gobble them down in chunks. He swallowed hard as he slid closer.

'Zade, oh my God, Zade!' Tina was crying as she gripped his hand so tightly that it almost stopped the flow of blood.

'I know, I know,' he said, but he was just as helpless. The surface they were on was smooth and polished, making their descent easy. Stopping wasn't an option, only an end.

Zade reached out and clutched Tina with both arms, tears welling up in his eyes. *It wouldn't take long*, he thought. He calculated the speed of them falling, plus the cog's fast cycle. They would be shredded in seconds. Perhaps if they were lucky they wouldn't feel much pain or, if they were very lucky, no pain at all. He wasn't convinced, though.

'Tina, I—' Before he could say any more, a huge bell rang out – twelve o'clock. *Dong!* They had to let go of one another and block their ears, both now falling separately.

They let out a scream of pain. If being devoured by ginormous cogs wasn't enough, they had to be deafened as well. In all the commotion, Zade, for a split second, saw that the rim of the clock face was jutting out a few centimetres from the surface of the wall. A flash of an idea seeped his mind. The pain in his ears was immense, but this was their only chance. With only seconds before they hit bottom he shot out his right arm and tensed and grabbed Tina around the waist with his left. He would only have one chance to grip that rim. It was really going to hurt if he could do it. The speed that they were travelling and the extra weight of his girlfriend was going to really wrench his arm. He had to prepare and hope that he wouldn't break it and that his grip was true.

Then, the split second his fingertips touched the small ledge, he latched on with all his heart! The pain in his arm was almost as bad as the pain in his ears but he held fast and snapped back like an elastic band. They stopped in mid-air and finally so did the ringing of the clock. Tina was still screaming and Zade could see why; the cogs were only centimetres from her feet!

Chapter 7

Obstacle

Pip got up and dusted down his T-shirt. He hissed in annoyance. There were white marks on his black top. He just hated dust; it was one of his little foibles. He went through the routine of vigorously patting himself down, grumbling as he did so.

'Oh, I ache all over. Give me a hand, Pip, will you?' Meadow winced. 'Where are we now? This place is unbelievable. If we're not in a room with a moving floor then it's a mental staircase or a long stupid slide. When will it all end?' she rattled on.

Pip wasn't really listening to her wining; he was back in concentration mode, the cogs grinding in his mind. He narrowed his eyes and chewed on his bottom lip.

'Shhh!' he interrupted. 'I can hear something.' He was staring at the wall but all his concentration was focused on sound.

'What are you doing?' she asked. She flicked her gaze from side to side and strained to hear too. She closed her eyes to give any distractions a wide birth. They listened intently and now, Meadow could hear it too. *Shoom-shoom... shoom-shoom... shoom-shoom...* It continued on in perfect harmony, like a slow electric fan or something, flying past your ears at moderate speed, back and forth.

'What is that?' Meadow probed and pointed into the distance. Far ahead there was a very large door.

'It's a door, Med,' Pip answered sarcastically, rolling his eyes. 'But I reckon we should definitely keep away from it. I don't want to know what's behind it.'

'Well that's going to be a bit impossible. It's the only way out of here, isn't it?' Meadow countered snidely, turning her head towards him. 'Wherever *here* is.' She paused. 'So there's no other direction we can go, is there, idiot?' she looked at him with deep penetrating brown eyes. He hated it when she was right. He liked being right.

'No need to be so condescending,' he rounded.

'Wooo, big words now too,' she teased.

He looked at her with contempt. He'd known about the door all along; he picked that up when they'd landed. He just didn't want to know what was beyond it. He realised that they couldn't go back either. The chute they'd just fallen from was out of reach, with no way of climbing up to it. They were really lucky that they hadn't sustained an injury from the fall.

Shoom-shoom… Shoom-shoom… Shoom-shoom… The sound continued to assault their ears. There was also a vibration that drilled through them.

'That noise is doing my head in,' Pip growled through gritted teeth. He held his hands against his ears.

'Well let's go and see what it is then,' Meadow retorted impatiently. 'Maybe it's a way out. I mean there has to be a way out, right?'

'I doubt that. Wherever we seem to go it feels as though we're heading further inside this place, you know? Rather than making our way out.'

'Shall we?' Meadow pointed in the direction that they knew they didn't want to go.

'If we must,' Pip relented.

Reluctantly, they began to steadily walk down the long corridor towards the door. By this point neither one knew who's heart was beating the fastest. Unexpectedly, the closer they got to the door, the more excited Pip became.

'This is incredible. It's like something out of a story – "Jack and the Beanstalk", maybe,' he tilted his head back. Meadow craned her neck too. The panel itself looked like a normal door except for its enormity.

'What?' Meadow was not one for reading and had never heard of the story. 'Jack and the what-Stalk?' she questioned.

'You don't know the story of "Jack and the Beanstalk?"' He paused and shook his head in disbelief,

'One of the most famous fairy tales ever written – good grief, woman.' He didn't pursue it any longer and focused.

There was a latch mechanism halfway up the door that involved a long metal bar that was nestled in a cradle. The bar itself was fixed at one end with a bolt, the other end was rested in the slot but was set through a metal sleeve. The sleeve would only just allow the bar to be picked up, release the door, and drop down again. Each of the components was made from brass and that brought a smile to Pip's face. He just loved old brass parts. But, ominously looking at the predicament, he sighed and ran his tongue under his front teeth.

'Oh my God, so one of us has to climb up there and release the latch while the other pulls back the door. Crap!' he cursed.

'What's a latch? I've never seen a latch before, Pip,' Meadow said curiously. Pip had, in his grandfather's old house in the country. Everything was authentic back then. But these days everything was plastic, cheaply made, and mass produced. The old ways used skilled craftsmen with a passion for their work.

'Those old mechanisms were all that they'd had years ago, Med,' he said proudly. He felt a warm sense of nostalgia, knowing things that normal teenagers didn't. But he still didn't want to know what lay ahead.

'Pip—Pip there you go again off into your own little world. Come on, snap out of it; we've got things to do, there's no time for all this memory rubbish.'

Meadow always thought of Pip as a dreamer. Everyone he met thought of him as a little dopey, but unbeknown to them he had a mind that worked like a calculator. Meadow didn't know this side of him. While others ran around and panicked he stayed quiet, working things out in his mind.

He knew what he had to do. He snapped back to reality.

'I'll have to get up there – but how?' he was mumbling to himself. He needed a ladder or steps of some sort. The door itself was wooden; it had two interlinked Z-shaped timbers. The middle crosspiece was the one timber that connected the two. He'd worked out what to do but how to get up the first part. He looked around for something to lean against the door so he could step on and climb up.

'Pip, what are you looking for?' Meadow asked, rubbing her forehead. Pip didn't have time to listen to his girlfriend, he had more important things to work out; he would need a ladder and the trajectory would have to be at a certain angle for him to climb. There was also the weight of the bar once he'd got up there. Could he lift it and could Meadow pull the huge door enough to set the latch free? To say there was a lot going through his head was an understatement.

'Pip—Pip! Whatever you're looking for there's nothing in here,' Meadow said impatiently. Pip wasn't listening; he was still looking around for a rope or something. After he'd exhausted his search, he stood and grimaced. *It's impossible,* he thought. *It can't be done.* He felt totally dejected and out of ideas, when…

'Pip!' Meadow's voice was calling him and he suddenly came round.

'What, Med? I haven't time for—' He'd been so wrapped up in his quest he'd forgotten about his girlfriend. Where the devil was she?

'Pip, Pip! Up here.' Meadow's voice sounded far away. He looked around and couldn't see her. He scratched at his chin, displacing his fluffy goatee.

'Meadow, where are you?' He began to panic. 'I can't see you, stop messing about.'

'I'm up here, you idiot,' she shouted from overhead. He looked directly up to where the latch was and saw her standing on the crosspiece of timber! His mouth dropped open to its fullest and his eyes to their widest. It was too much for him to take in.

'Huh, how did you get—When did you get—' He was ranting.

'I climbed up. I'm in the gymnastics team, remember?' she said proudly. He felt a little silly.

'B—but, all my calculations and theories.' He was mumbling to himself again. He was also supposed to be the brains, but obviously he wasn't, and as far as gymnastics was concerned he preferred to keep his feet squarely on the ground.

'Some people think and some people do,' she said smugly from her perch.

'All right, you've made your point; do you think you can lift the latch?' he shouted up sharply, sort of hoping she couldn't just for pride's sake, but knowing deep down that she was totally capable. *She's going to be unbearable after*, he thought.

'I don't know, I'll have a go,' she called back. Meadow knelt onto the long plank of wood. It was just wide enough to settle on. She tentatively reached down, keeping her balance. There was a small brass knob on the side of the metal bar so she slid her left hand carefully underneath and cupped it in her palm. She gripped with splayed fingers and it felt cold to the touch, sending a chill through her whole body. It felt smooth and she tensed herself before taking the weight. She counted to three and braced herself – clenched her eyes shut and yanked at it but it didn't move. It didn't even shift a little.

She gasped in defeat and felt as though a huge weight was pressing down on her. She could feel Pip's eyes on her and didn't want to let herself or him down. She closed her eyes and tried again, this time with as much force as she could muster. It did jiggle a bit in its holster, giving her a whiff of hope but that was all. It was of no use with only one hand on it.

'Damn it, come on.' She willed it to move further. 'Don't let me down now, hand of mine,' she mumbled. She dreaded the next bit, but knew what she had to do and shook her head in denial. She had to use both hands, but that meant that her balance was going to be compromised. It was a long way down too.

She tried not to look, preparing herself for the next part. *Oh, why do things have to be so difficult?* the words whizzing around in her head.

'What's happening?' Pip's voice broke her concentration and made her lurch forward and almost slip and fall. She gripped and steadied herself.

'Will you shut up, you bloody idiot! I nearly fell then, dopey,' she screamed down at him, spittle oozing from between her teeth. She sucked it back in.

'Sorry, Meadow, but what are you doing?' He looked up and wished he'd had a pair of binoculars. 'I'm at a loss down here and can't see anything.'

'Well come up here then and you can see firsthand, or just shut up and let me get on with it,' she repeated angrily, her voice echoing back as if in a large cave.

'All right, I'm sorry, I'll be quiet,' he whimpered and subconsciously put his finger to his lips.

Meadow again leaned to her right and spread her knees at a wider angle. She reached out with her right hand and grasped the back of her left, shifting her weight even more to her right side. She interlocked her fingers and braced herself once more, closed her eyes and breathed out.

'Come on, girl,' she encouraged herself and gripped and pulled as hard as she could. This time she felt the weight lift. She kept her wits about her and continued to lift back into her body. Pip could see the latch moving, even from a distance. He realised at that moment that he was in the wrong place and ran towards the edge of the door. This is where he should have been waiting anyway.

'Don't let go, Meadow.' He panted as he jogged. Could he pull the door open? He definitely couldn't let Meadow down at this point.

'I've… go… it… up…' Meadow's voiced strained from above. 'Pull the bloody door, Pip, for God's sake. I can't hold it much longer,' she blasted angrily.

He grabbed the edge of the wood with both hands and pulled with all his heart. It seemed to move very slowly. There was an echoed clang as the latch fell and hit metal. There was a pause; Pip couldn't look. He was too terrified. Was it back inside its slot or did she manage to release it?

'It worked!' Meadow shouted down to him and Pip's whole body deflated like a football with a puncture.

Chapter 8

Hanging On

Zade's grip was getting weaker. He was holding his own body weight as well as his girlfriend's, who dangled precariously below. Tina's screams shrieked through the air like a machine gun, adding to Zade's headache.

'Teen, stop screeching in my ear,' he protested as she frantically held her arms around his neck, almost strangling him. The more she fretted, though, the heavier she seemed to get. 'Stop wriggling, Teen. It's – argh! – hard enough holding on as it is,' he grunted through clenched teeth.

'I don't want to die,' she bleated, her voice hoarse and dashed with fear.

'Neither do I,' Zade responded. His fingers were at a point where they didn't have any feeling at all. He foolishly peered through half-shut eyes to see if he was still holding on. He did have both hands on the ledge. How he managed to do it he still didn't know. The ear-piercing clock chimes had stopped and Tina had quietened down too, to his relief, but the continued ringing of countless rotating cogs, in fast sequence, sang out with an almost hypnotic but deadly quality.

Tina looked down and trembled; her feet were dangling within metres of the metal teeth. She tried to swallow but her mouth was totally dry. Her breathing quickened.

'D—don't wriggle, Teen, p—please keep still.' Zade strained and grunted through teeth clamped shut, the sweat pouring down his face and burning his eyes. His palms were getting clammy and he knew it would only be a matter of minutes before he let go.

'Teen, is there anything you can grab hold of? My grip is getting weaker.' The words came out of his mouth stretched and strained. She tentatively swept her gaze from left to right.

'No, there's nothing.' She was whimpering as she said it. 'Don't let me fall, Zade… Please don't let me fall!' There were tears glistening in her eyes and a taut mask of fear etched on her face. She knew death was only moments away.

'Tina,' Zade said simply; his voice had a tone of finality about it. He paused before uttering his next statement. 'I can't hold on much longer.' His voice was one of desparation. 'When I let—'

'Zade—Zade, the second hand,' Tina interrupted, a spark of hope in her words. Look—look, it's within my grasp, I think.'

'What, Teen?' Zade closed his eyes in concentration pushing all his energy to his fingers.

'I'll grab it next time around and, with a bit of luck, it will pull me up. Just hold on a bit longer – you'll see, it'll work. Please, Zade, just hold on and maybe we can get out of this.' She seemed really focused.

This gave Zade a boost and he felt stronger for the next handful of seconds; his eyes were fully shut as he concentrated praying, if he was honest with himself.

'Tina, what's happening?' he whispered calmly. He didn't have to wait any longer; Tina had measured the next cycle and reached out her hand. The slim second hand was approaching and with her heart beating at a phenomenal rate she reached out. She grasped it with one huge lunge. Zade felt the jerk and his heart skipped a beat. He tensed and thought he was going to fall, but he was still there. Second by second, literally, it began lifting her up and easing the weight off Zade's arms. He felt instant relief, as if floating, but he daren't let go. How he was still holding on he didn't know, but he kept on focusing.

At a quarter to the hour, Tina had let go of Zade's neck altogether, and by the time it reached the number eleven she slid down its shaft and stood on the central pin.

'Zade, come on – you grab it next time round,' she urged. He looked up and for the first time he could see she was safe, at least for now. From where she was positioned she couldn't reach down to help him without falling. She was even smiling at him and that gave a warm feeling inside. Zade could see the long arm approaching. Did he have enough strength in his fingers, arms, shoulders, or heart to reach up and grab freedom? There were a lot of variables.

'Zade, it's almost there, grab it, come on,' she called to him.

'I don't know if I can, Teen.' The defeatist tone in his voice irked her.

'Zade, grab the bloody thing – NOW!' This seemed to wake him up. It was above him and slowly making its way past, back to the top. He took one stab at it with his left hand and, without even thinking, latched on. The pain in his arm and hand was immense but he didn't have time to ponder as it pulled him up. His right hand slipped from its grip on the ledge and dangled by his side, limply. He knew he couldn't hold on with just his one hand, and so willed his right arm to move. He had his eyes clenched shut and lifted his right arm, tracing its way to the left. He gripped on with both hands now until he could eventually slide down to where Tina stood.

He followed her lead and eventually they were both balancing on the centre shaft. She had to hold him upright as to avoid the second hand colliding with them. The last thing they wanted now was to be knocked off and fall to their doom. Zade stood, vigorously rubbing his shoulders and arms, and gently flexing his fingers to get the blood flowing again. The aching was unbearable and he felt like crying, but held back in front of his girlfriend.

'Awww,' he cringed, as his face creased up.

'Zade, you all right?' Tina rubbed his arms to help him. 'You were amazing,' she gushed.

'Ah, shut up,' he said, embarrassed. After a little while things felt as though they were getting easier and so Zade relaxed.

'Oh, that feels better,' he said, rolling his shoulders and expelling a breath of air; it was the best feeling in the world. He rolled his shoulders again, twisting his neck from side to side, loosening up his previously taut muscles.

'Look, out it's coming again,' Tina said, watching as the hand fast approached.

'Oh yeah.' He'd almost forgotten about the rotation, too submerged in easing his pain. He began to refocus. 'That was something that I don't ever want to go through again.'

'How are we going to get off this thing, Zade?' Tina asked looking ominously at the churning, menacing cogs below.

Zade wasn't listening; he was scouting out any possibility he could find to escape.

'Zade—Zade, here it comes again,' Tina warned. The second hand continued on its dutiful clockwork dance. A point of interest flickered into Zade's vision.

'Tina, look over there.' He pointed to what looked like a boxed ledge with a square hole in the top.

'What do you think it is?' she asked.

'I don't know, but it could be a way out. We have to try something to get off here.'

'How do we get to it though?' she asked. 'And if we can, what if it isn't a way out?'

'God, you can be so negative sometimes. I don't know all the answers, Teen, but I do know that we can't stay here forever. Down is death for sure. We're both going to eventually get tired and fall asleep. When that happens, we'll fall – simple as that.'

They looked at the metal grinders below. The thought of being chewed into tiny pieces scratched its way through Tina's head and she shivered.

'That's the only way out as far as I can see,' he said, pointing again, and she looked at him and nodded.

'How do we do this?' she asked, cluelessly. 'You got a plan. Come on, you've always got some kind of plan, right?' Zade was watching the movement of the clock. Once more the small hand came around in its silent vigil.

'If we wait until twelve forty and then slowly shimmy along the length of the minute hand—' he said with confidence as a plan had hatched.

'Yes?' She was looking back at him with a dark sense of fear.

'Then between the number eight and nine we can jump off onto the ledge.' He smiled and expected a nod of approval.

'Jump?' was all she answered as she ran her tongue over her top lip. 'I don't know. What, just leap off?'

'Yeah, you know.' He made a little jerky movement and almost went off balance. 'You're a netball player,' he grinned. 'Don't they jump all the time in netball?'

'You're an idiot,' she answered. 'Of course I used to jump in netball.'

'Well, it should be nothing to you,' he said with relish, 'Teen the Netball Queen.'

'Meadow is the gymnast. I used to play netball, but there's no ball and definitely no net, is there?' she retorted.

'And there's not much time left here either?' he said pessimistically, before looking down again. 'Or,' he added, 'that second hand will out-wit us eventually knock us off.'

'All right, all right, I get it. We'll jump!' Tina said finally. She'd blurted out the words but didn't believe in any of them. So they waited and concentrated. By twelve thirty-five the angle was still too great.

It felt like an eternity but twelve forty finally arrived. Tina sort of wanted it to happen and when it did, didn't want it to.

Her head was all over the place. The two of them mounted the arm, Zade first and Tina behind as they slid toward the narrower end. It was way more difficult this time around. The second hand was out of their line of sight for two thirds of the minute. By the time it made its way back to them, they were concentrating so much they'd forgotten about it. The only clues they had to its arrival was a gentle shudder as it approached and the fact that it came from below. This meant that they could actually see it coming.

'Incoming!' Zade shouted repeatedly in military fashion. They then had to stop and lean to one side, narrowly avoiding the slicing blow of the giant sword. Tina was slowing down and Zade looked back to see if she was OK.

'Teen, come on, it's quarter to twelve and we should already have jumped off by now,' he demanded, worried that they might have missed their chance.

'I'm trying, I'm trying,' she screamed breathlessly in frustration. 'I can't go any faster.'

'The longer we leave it the further we'll have to jump,' he rasped with distaste.

Zade finally got to the end and he was shocked to see what the gap really looked like close up. The other side was a lot further away than he'd anticipated… and getting further away by the minute. Tina slid up behind him and he could feel her trembling body and hot breath on his neck. By now it was in between forty-five and fifty. Zade stood up and balanced himself, and was just about to jump when the second hand stealthily knocked him off. They'd forgotten about its rotation! He fell with a scream as Tina watched on helplessly.

'Oh my God, the second hand,' she screeched. He didn't land on the ledge as planned, but managed to grip its rim. His hands were weaker this time and his forearms were burning and aching at the same time. But unfortunately for him there were no footholds to help him climb and push his way up. He couldn't turn to encourage his girlfriend to jump either, and hung there feebly.

Tina stood up and waited for the second hand to pass again. 'You're not taking me too,' she whispered.

On the stroke of twelve fifty she jumped. She didn't calculate the jump, nor did she think about the consequence of missing the ledge. She just leapt and hoped for the best; she had nothing to lose.

She landed on the ledge perfectly, like a Russian gymnast.

Unfortunately for Zade, she did land on one of his hands and he screamed out in pain. She'd realised what she'd done and quickly leaned over. Grabbing him with all the might she could muster she pulled him up to safety. They sat each side of the hole and said nothing for a while. This was the first time they'd actually sat down. They both relaxed and enjoyed the feeling of rest, with their eyes closed. Without knowing it, they dropped off into a dreamy sleep for a short while.

Tina was the first to open her eyes and sighed when she saw where they were. She'd hoped that it had actually been a dream, and they could all go home, but it was not to be.

'Zade... Zade, wake up,' she said, nudging him gently.

'Cup of tea and some toast, Mum,' he mumbled as he stirred.

'Wake up, Zade, I'm not your mum,' Tina scolded. He opened his eyes a crack and let out a sigh.

'Oh, are we still here?' His reaction was the same as hers.

'I'm afraid we are, mate,' she replied despairingly. Then the pain of everything kicked in and he sighed again. He looked over at the clock and then below at the cogs.

'At least we're still alive,' he said with gratitude.

'We do have to be thankful for that,' Tina said.

'What do we have here then?' Zade sort of questioned himself more than anything.

When they looked inside the hole, both their hearts sank. There appeared to be a long ladder disappearing into the vastness of many levels of platforms. It was a void of which there seemed to be no end.

'How did we get into this mess?' Zade asked, shaking his head in confusion.

'I've no idea, but I want to go home now,' Tina replied.

'Me too, this place is all one-way, there's never any going back. Have you noticed that?' Zade mumbled to himself.

'What?' Tina asked.

'Well,' he piped up, 'wherever we've gone so far, there is only one escape route – or death! This guy Darke must be one weird person. When he created this house he wanted entertainment and a means for his victims to get out too, if they made it, of course. Well, I don't intend to be his puppet forever. Come on, let's get out of here.'

He got up, filled with determination, and climbed down into the hole, with Tina hot on his heels.

Chapter 9

Noise

Meadow, her task done, carefully but with athletic skill, scuttled down the wooden framework to the floor. She made it look almost effortless. Pip smiled as she approached him and he arched his eyebrows in surprise.

'That was amazing, Med,' he gushed. 'I would never have guessed you could do that.'

'We don't know much about each other, do we?' she remarked with a hint of regret. 'It's ridiculous, we've been going out together a while.'

'I guess we don't but there's still time – you know? When we get out of this place.' He answered with the same sense of misgiving. They looked into one another's eyes for a moment, then, as quick as the moment had appeared, it dissipated, leaving them both wondering.

'What's inside there?' Pip continued, changing the subject completely. The noise was much more prominent now. Shoom-shoom… Shoom-shoom…

'There is only one way to find out,' Meadow suggested, but Pip was already walking towards the gap. 'Is this wise?' she asked trepidatiously also knowing there was no other way.

'Come on, we have to find your brother and his girlfriend and get out of this stupid house,' he added venomously. They walked through the small gap between the door and the framework and entered the next room. The big door eased back into place and they turned when they heard the latch fall back into its cradle with a clunk. It felt so final.

'Jesus, I hate this place,' Pip said grating his teeth. 'This guy knows exactly where we are at all times, but I don't see any cameras,' he puzzled, sweeping the area with close scrutiny. 'He's clever, but even evil geniuses come unstuck at some point.'

'We're never going to get out of here, are we?' Meadow began sobbing, her resilient side melting away.

'Yes we are, come on, we can't let him beat us,' he retorted grabbing her hand and walking through. 'Don't let him win, Med,' he said as he gently squeezed. This made her feel a little stronger and the warmth of companionship filled her.

The corridor was again long and dimly lit, with burning torches fixed to the walls. The flames spat and hissed as they passed by, as if the torches were repulsed by the children's appearance. The passageway itself was arched and the whole thing made of metal. The floor, ceiling, and walls were studded with big rivets that must have held the iron plate together, or so Pip assumed. There was also a sequence of sections that were set out three to four metres apart, like stepping from room to room.

'Man, this has got the feel of being inside a submarine or something. How can a house of bricks and mortar have a place like this inside?' Pip was taking in all his surroundings.

'It's cool.' The engineering of the building overwhelmed his sense of learning new things.

'I don't think it's cool, Pip; I don't like it at all. In fact, it's like something out of a dungeon.' She shuddered at the thought.

Pip was more relaxed now and quite enjoying himself. They came to a bend that curved off to their right. The sound was fast becoming louder as they advanced and, not only that, they could feel a vibration in the ground underfoot.

Meadow stopped and Pip carried on. He realised after a few steps that he was on his own and turned.

'What's the matter? Come on.' He beckoned with a wave of his hand. 'We have to go on.'

'I don't know if I want to see what we're up against,' she said, fear pouring over her like a shower.

'I don't think we have a choice, Med. Really, I don't.' Pip raised his eyebrow as he said it and walked back. He put his arm around her shoulder for support. 'You know we can't go back and maybe Tina and Zade are just up ahead.'

Meadow thought for a moment, she then wrinkled her nose and breathed in. 'You handled that door with ease, girlfriend,' he said, totally looking out of place by trying to sound trendy. She blurted a giggle.

'Girlfriend!' she responded.

'All right, all right, I was trying to be hip. I heard that somewhere and thought it would work… obviously it didn't,' he said feeling hopelessly lost at his remark.

'Only girls use "girlfriend" as part of a conversation, it's totally American,' she grinned, feeling lighter in the moment.

This changed her attitude and she breathed hard and licked her lips. 'OK, I'm ready, I think. Let's go find out what that damn noise is.'

The pair edged round the corner and saw, in plain view, what had been hounding them for the last hour. It took their breath away. They looked into one another's eyes and grinned nervously.

'Oh my God,' Meadow squeaked.

The sound was emitted by two swinging pendulums. They were suspended inside what looked like a huge grandfather clock. The pendulums' arms rose high into the stratosphere.

'What's with this guy? Have we shrunk all of a sudden?' Pip asked himself, but he couldn't be heard above the sound of swishing. The arms themselves were made of what looked like solid brass. They were shaped like large blades. Three quarters the way down each one a circular disc with a painted end was fitted. They were lethal and reminded Pip of two huge swords. If circumstances were different he would stay and admire the craftsmanship but this wasn't a field trip. And these things weren't there to be admired. They were an obstacle that had to be passed and without being killed if possible. Pip gulped hard before he moved on.

Beyond the clock workings was a ladder, that also seemed to ascend high into the top part of the clock, but they couldn't see the clock face or anything past the darkness. The foreboding sound of each swing made Meadow and Pip shudder. The closer they got, the more deadly the situation felt.

'We have to get past these, don't we?' Meadow shouted, the sound taking her conversation with it. 'And then what?' He peered back at her and took a deep breath before he spoke. His heart felt as though it would explode before he finished talking.

'Look, Meadow,' he called out dryly, 'I know as much as you. I'm scared too, you know. It's obvious we can't go back. We have to negotiate these things.'

'What?' she screeched back.

'We have to get past this and then…' He stopped shouting and strained to hear something. 'Hey, what's that?' He narrowed his eyes in concentration. Meadow looked at him and closed her eyes for a moment, and tried to shut out the continuous bombardment of the clock. There it was. A high-pitched squeal that became prominent and then swept away.

'I… I think that's Tina,' Meadow cried with great relief. 'She sounds as if she's in trouble.'

There was definitely screaming coming from above. If it wasn't for the heavy sound of the clock they would have heard it earlier. Their reluctance was replaced by the quest of seeing their friends and siblings again.

'We have to help them,' Pip swiftly cut in, his voice almost cracking under the pressure of bellowing. The pendulums were the least of their problems now!

'How are we going to do this, Pip?' Meadow shouted in the din. Pip had no idea – it was going to be all timing.

'We have to run,' he said, then realising he'd spoken softly. 'I haven't time to calculate things. We're going to have to run and hope for the best.' She looked at him with a squint, unable to hear.

'I said, we're going to have to run straight through it,' he bellowed, his chest heaving as he spoke, 'and hope for the best.' His eyes flared with fear and, his mouth resembled a cave opening.

'What? No technical jargon about trajectory or split-second timing or the wind has to be a certain direction? That's all you've come up with is – we run?' She knew this already but was hoping for a different solution. Pip always had a genius plan but this time there wasn't one.

Another scream cut through the air like a sabre. Pip looked up as if he could see where it was coming from. But, when he looked back at the swinging pendulums, he gasped, his eyes on stalks. Meadow was running straight for them! He almost couldn't shout.

'Meadow, stop!' he cried, but it was no use, she was almost there. She ran head on and, at the last part, even closed her eyes. Pip could barely watch as she hit the dual blades at exactly the right time and slipped right through the middle. He held his breath and then gushed. It was perfect; they hadn't touched her and she was through with all her limbs intact.

She tripped and fell flat on her face on the other side. There could only have been centimetres between her and death. What was she thinking? But he also knew there was really no other way.

'You idiot,' he bellowed. 'You could have been killed.'

'I'm fine,' she called beckoning him over with a wave.

'I know, I know,' he said, more to himself than anything. His heart was racing and his mouth was dry. When he pulled back to get some air into his lungs, his breath seemed to escape him. He felt a build-up of sweat on his upper lip and his hands were clammy. Meadow was calling him but it felt as if he was watching a film in slow motion, with no sound accompanying it. It felt like there was a little person inside his chest beating a gong. He tensed and put his left foot ahead of his right. He could hardly think, never mind anything else. He felt faint – it's now or never.

He suddenly jerked into a sprint and ran for all he was worth.

Thud, thud, thud.

He didn't like this; he didn't do things like this. He was always prepared, but he had no choice. He would normally work this out scientifically before even attempting such a thing but he sped on anyway. He closed his eyes as he entered and felt something clip his heel. It flipped him around in a three hundred and sixty degree spin. He was disorientated, the world rushing past like trees flashing past a train carriage window. He closed his eyes, but was still standing. He could feel the sweep of wind from both sides now and the loud swooshing sound all around him. He could also barely hear Meadow calling frantically from beyond.

Where was he? He tentatively opened his eyes a crack. All his fears gushed forward into one huge lump. He was indeed in between the two blades, with barely centimetres between him and each one. One slip and that would be the end. He began to tremble as the adrenalin took over. He couldn't stay here long. It would only be a matter of time before he buckled and became mincemeat. He sucked in air, closed his eyes once more, and counted the rhythm. There was only really one blade he had to worry about as long as he didn't stick out his butt too far to escape. He even grinned at that point, a nervous, totally scared grin. He concentrated and stepped forward. All he heard was a scream and felt a tugging sensation and a cold rush of air against his cheek. It felt good and he began to breathe again. He rolled over onto his back and opened his eyes. Meadow was standing over him with a huge grin on her face.

'You idiot,' she whispered and gently kissed him on his parched lips. 'Get up, Pip, we've got a ladder to climb.' With that she was already making her way up.

Chapter 10

Middle Ground

They couldn't see too far down into the gloom but didn't really want to look anyway, wondering what evil lay ahead. There was a ladder and then a platform and possibly beyond that more ladders and more platforms. They assumed the whole structure was a vast network of metal.

'I'll bet it's a long way down. This house must be huge,' said Zade, peering into the black and doing so made him feel downbeat.

'Don't you understand by now, Zade?' Tina panted with every step she took as she descended the rungs above him. 'This house is all in the mind of that stupid Lord Darke guy. Somehow he has the magic to create anything.' She paused and whispered, 'We'll never get out of here.' A deep sadness filled the pit of her stomach and she chewed her bottom lip.

'Teen, don't say that. Look he must have a weakness, we'll find it. I'll find it,' Zade insisted with confidence. 'He won't beat us, come on, chin up.'

They continued to descend a couple more levels until Zade came to a stop.

'Zade, what are you doing?' Tina asked when she almost stamped her right foot on his hand. 'Tell me when you're going to stop, won't you? I'm working blind here.'

'I don't know, it's just a feeling. Let's rest here for a little bit so I can think,' he said, not sounding at all confident. He stepped off the ladder and on to the platform.

Tina took the few steps down and climbed off too. She rubbed the base of her back and continued further down to her calves. They ached from all the stretching on the steel rungs. She rolled her shoulders to free the taught muscles. Then she eased her head from side to side, it felt good. Feeling a little more relaxed she rested her hands on the cold rail that surrounded them. She leaned over and peered as far as she could below. It was annoying, after two or so levels everything was still swallowed up by darkness. She pulled back, held onto the rail for support again, and looked up. It felt as though they were in a tunnel and the only source of light was the pin-prick they'd left behind, but that was way up there now. Her neck began to ache again so she straightened up. She looked at her boyfriend propped up against the ladder staring into the darkness. He didn't have a clue what to do, she could tell. She felt obligated to ease his troubled mind.

'Zade, it'll be all—' But she was cut short! There was movement below, shuffling far beneath them, it caught them by surprise.

'Zade! Tina! Is that you?' The voice echoed from the blackness and seemed to rise through the vastness of the cavern.

'Yes, Meadow, are you all right?' Zade called back, this new commotion sparking him into life. 'Is Pip there with you too?'

'Yes we're fine, we're coming up,' Meadow shouted, her voice almost lost in the confusion of the echoes. 'There's no way out down at the bottom.'

'There's no way out at the top either,' Zade called back despondently.

They waited until Meadow and Pip made it to their level. Everyone was reunited and hugs and kisses were handed out freely all round.

'God, I've missed you sis,' Zade said, grabbing his little sister in a bear hug.

'Aww, that's sweet,' she responded in her normal level of sarcasm.

'All right, Med, you know I care about you, no need for the remarks,' he quipped.

'I never thought I'd see you two again,' Pip chipped in.

'All this climbing has made me really thirsty,' Zade commented.

'Me too,' Pip said.

'Unbelievable.' Meadow was staring and shaking her head.

'What's the matter, Med?' Tina asked innocently, looking slightly confused at her comment.

'Look over there.' She pointed to the corner of the platform they were on. There, laid out on the floor, were four bottles of water and some snacks in the shape of crisps and chocolate.

'But how?' Pip half asked.

'Yeah, how?' Zade asked. 'That lot wasn't there a minute ago, I'm sure of it.'

'No, it wasn't, I would have seen it,' Tina added. 'What's going on here? I told you, Zade, all these things are in this guy's mind, somehow. There's no way he could have put them there without us seeing him do it.'

'Don't drink or eat it in case it's poisoned,' Meadow advised.

'What?' Zade looked at his sister in disbelief. 'If this guy Darke wanted us dead, Med, he could have done it right at the beginning, couldn't he? I mean, he has the power to do all this,' Zade pointed out. 'He's just playing us. I suppose he could press a little button wherever he is and this whole structure could collapse. There wouldn't be any need to poison us. Look.' Zade walked over to the corner and picked up a random bottle to demonstrate. He snapped it open and drank willingly. He stopped suddenly and began gagging and spluttering. He put his hand around his throat, choking, and looked at them with real fear in his eyes. The girls rushed over to help him and he just smiled. Tina and Meadow realised they'd been tricked and both of them hit him on each shoulder.

'Stop it,' he recoiled with a grin.

'You idiot,' they scolded in unison.

'Hey, hey, take it easy,' he pleaded, still grinning. Pip didn't move a muscle, shutting his eyes in disbelief.

'Don't do that again. I mean it,' Tina said.

'It was only a joke, sorry. The water is fine.' He picked up a couple and handed them to the girls. Pip went over and grabbed one for himself. Soon they were all drinking and devouring crisps and chocolate in a frenzy.

'I didn't realise how hungry I was,' Meadow spluttered in between mouthfuls.

'Me too,' Tina responded, covering her mouth in a very ladylike fashion.

'Where now?' Zade spoke reluctantly. 'We're stuck in the middle. Down leads to nowhere and up leads to nowhere.' He stopped and looked over at the ladder with curiosity but it wasn't there anymore. There was, however, a solid wall in its place. In fact, none of them were on a metal platform at all anymore. They were all standing inside a long corridor.

'What, when did this happen?' Zade tried to make sense of it all. 'I was just looking at… Oh, I don't know.'

'What is this all about?' Meadow growled.

'This is doing my head in,' Tina spat.

'This is fantastic,' Pip added, looking impressed. 'All this took place in seconds. This man is a genius.'

'This man is a lunatic,' Zade cut in. 'This is not right. He has too much power at his disposal. What is he?'

'I'm with you on that one, Zade,' Tina agreed. 'He's capable of anything.'

'My congratulations.' They all recognised the voice straight away; it was definitely Lord Darke. 'You have succeeded much further than I could have dreamed. Well done.' Tina tried to see where his voice was coming from. Meadow swallowed hard. Zade gritted his teeth in revulsion and Pip calmly stood and listened.

'Let us out, please let us out,' Tina pleaded. 'I can't stay here any longer. My parents will be worried, they'll call the police.'

'I'm sorry, but I'm afraid I can't let that happen yet.' Lord Darke's voice seemed to come from everywhere, 'I have things for you to do first,' he continued.

'What things? Haven't we done enough for you?' Meadow bellowed.

'But you will eventually let us out?' Zade asked with hope.

'Well not all of you, some must perish. There are always casualties in war, you know,' he said flippantly.

'Uh, what do you mean?' Pip asked, now speaking up. 'Some of us will die? What war? We're not in any war with you? We've done nothing to deserve this. We are just on some kind of bike ride, and only need help. If you have a quarrel with someone else, then why do we have to be involved? We never asked for this. We just want to go home. You can't keep us here.'

'Ah, but I can. It's all part of the game, my game. Darke by name and dark by nature,' he chuckled, his voice tapering off. There was a pause but the voice didn't continue.

'You can't just say that and go, you coward!' Pip was ranting.

Zade stood grim faced and looked at the others. 'We've survived this far, we can make it, all of us,' he said adamantly. 'All right, where does this corridor lead? Come on, you lot, let's stick together this time.' Zade strolled off, a bewildered group of teenagers following. They marched to the end of an empty corridor and out once again onto the balcony overlooking the foyer.

'Wow, we've made it.' A great smile filled Tina's face, a smile of joy and relief. 'The door that led us in here is only at the bottom of the stairs – look.' She pointed excitedly at the entrance. 'Come on while we can. We can get out of here right now.'

'Hold it, Teen. Just hold on a minute,' Zade said sceptically. 'This is way too easy. I don't trust him. This is definitely not right.' He stared straight ahead. He bit his bottom lip trying to make sense of things.

'I don't care, Zade, I want to go home and there's our way out.' Tina was focused as she pointed to the front door.

'He's right, Tina,' Pip said. 'This guy is way too cunning for it to be that easy. You can't trust him. You've already seen what he's done to us. This has got to be a trap.'

'I agree,' Meadow said in Pip's defence. 'I don't normally agree with Pip, never mind my brother, but it's just too... easy! Can't you see, he's only just told us that we won't all make it out, and now he's giving us our escape route! Especially after all he's put us through. No, we must take it easy. Let's just think about this.' Meadow shook her head doubtfully. Tina paused for a moment; her mind was a whirl of confusion. She rubbed her left hand over her brow and clenched her eyes shut.

'All right,' she said, just nodding. 'I'm with you.'

'OK.' Zade took a deep breath before he spoke again. 'He's capable of anything so let's not split up this time. We are stronger together. Let's take the stairs on the left slowly and make our way to the door.'

'Why?' Pip asked.

'Why what?' Zade retorted with a feeling of agitation.

'Why the stairs on the left?' he asked again.

'Does it really matter?' Meadow interrupted.

'Well it does to me,' Pip rounded.

'OK then.' Zade raised his hands in submission and then gestured to the other side. 'The right side then. Is that OK?'

But none of the debate mattered because, as they were arguing, Tina was already halfway down the left stairwell.

'I'm not listening any more. I'm going now.'

'Tina, what are you doing?' Zade bellowed.

'Making my own informed decision,' she replied simply and bounded downwards.

'Come on, let's go,' Meadow said to the others as she followed Tina.

'Stop!' Pip screeched out. He looked pale and worried. 'It's a trap, I'm sure of it.'

'Oh, what now?' Tina turned to face him as she was about to walk onto the tiles.

'The floor, it – I don't know,' he blurted in astonishment. 'There's… something strange happening.' The words were strained as he stuttered.

'What… what do you mean, you "don't know"?' Tina barked back angrily.

'Just wait a minute, I've got a feeling there's danger,' Pip persisted. 'Please, just wait.'

'I've had enough of this, I'm going.' With that, Tina turned and stepped off the last step and onto the floor. But she didn't step onto it like she should have done. Instead she immediately sank into muddied tiles, like falling into a vat of quicksand. The floor was not solid, it distorted into liquid. Everyone looked on in horror because she was quickly being immersed and swallowed by the ground. No one was more shocked that Tina herself. She realised how stubborn she had been, but it was way too late now.

Meadow stood panicking; she moved forward and was about to lean over and try to grab her friend when Zade pulled her back. Meadow screamed and burst into tears. 'Let me get her, leave me alone, we can't leave her,' she cried.

'No, Med, you and Pip hold my arm. Come on quickly. I've got a much longer reach than both of you. I can get her, listen to me.'

Meanwhile, Tina was screaming and thrashing around, but the more she panicked the easier it was for the ground to suck her down. The look of fear on her face was torturous.

'Help, Zade, hel—' But her torso was already under. It was only her head that was on the surface and that too was fast disappearing. Zade speedily knelt on the edge of the stairs and was almost touching the mud himself. He stretched out for all he was worth.

'Oh my God, she's going down too fast,' he mumbled. There were tears in his eyes as he flexed his hand and only managed to get his fingertips to her hair. He was breathing hard, gasping for air. He couldn't lose her, he loved her. He eased back slightly and heaved out again with every fibre of his body, willing himself to reach her.

'Come on!' He strained as hard as he could, sweat pouring down his face, sinews at breaking point. He had managed to get a little further than before but even that wasn't enough.

'Tina, grab my arm, come on.' He was frantic. 'Tina, hold on, I'll grab you. Please—please hold on.'

He was desperate; tears were pouring down his face and stung his eyes. Snot poured out from his nostrils and dribbled off his chin. It finally dawned on him but he couldn't accept it. *My God, where did she go?* he thought. She couldn't answer him, it was too late; she was gone, sucked into the sick imagination of Darke's evil mind.

'Tina! Tina! Come back! Please come back! *Please!*' An emptiness that he couldn't describe filled his whole heart. He felt sick and drained and a failure.

'Oh my God.' He chocked the words.

'She's gone, Zade.'

He heard his sister's dry, smokey voice whisper from behind. 'She's gone.'

He wiped the back of his hand across his mouth and bit hard. More tears came, but he couldn't accept that she was gone forever.

Chapter 11

Three

Zade, tears still rolling down his face, tried frantically to dip his hand into the mud, but he couldn't. It wasn't mud any more; it was a solid floor, back to its original marble. But he'd known in his heart of hearts that was going to happen. Darke opened things up and closed them off at random. How he did it he didn't know, but that was of no consequence now. He pulled away from the others and flopped onto his stomach. He urgently scratched and then pounded hard on the tiles, trying to make a crack, a dent – anything!

'Stop it—stop it, Zade,' Meadow shrieked in anguish. 'You'll hurt yourself.' She was crying, warm bulbous tears streaking down her smooth skin. Pip was next to her, also shocked and upset by the grave situation but without telling them, intrigued too. Zade again desperately tried to dig his nails into the floor and find some way of rescuing her. But it was no use.

'Why?' he wailed, his emotions escaping their normally cool exterior. 'Why her?' His voice reverberated into the great vastness of the house. 'You could've taken me instead. I don't understand, why are you doing this? Why don't you come and take me? Let Tina come back, and take me. She didn't harm anyone.'

He was sobbing and his tears pooled on the glossy surface and mirrored his look of anguish. Meadow fell to the ground and hugged her brother, sobbing uncontrollably as she did so.

'Zade, I'm so sorry,' she said as she finally let him go. Nobody moved from that spot for a while. After the sadness came reflection and hatred. There was mostly quiet after that except for the ticking of clocks in the background. The annoying tick-tick-tick that drove Zade mad, another form of torture Darke had devised. He burst up from the floor and rushed over to the nearest one. All the anger and pain had built up inside like a cork in a bottle. He let all his frustration and grief escape as he gripped the side panel of the antique timepiece. With one huge surge of energy he pulled the wooden clock over. As if in slow motion it toppled and fell face to the floor. The excruciating sound of smashing glass and splintering wood filled the air. Meadow screamed as she and Pip grasped their ears to ease the deafening sound. Zade stood, chest heaving and fire in his eyes; it was stupid and irresponsible but it made him feel a little better. When the last echoes died away, Meadow spoke.

'We're not going to get out of here, are we?' she said dryly. Dark patches had appeared under her eyes, a mixture of redness and streaked mascara.

'I don't know, I don't care now, either, not without Tina. Who the hell is this Lord Epacseon Darke anyway?' Zade cried, angry and tired and filled with a loss. Nothing mattered now. But then he realised that he still had to be strong for his little sister.

'I don't think we're going to be able to get out of here, full stop,' Pip said out of his silence. They looked at him with distaste.

'How do you know that?' Zade spat back.

Pip peered back innocently. 'I've only just worked out his stupid name.

'What—What do you mean?' Zade didn't understand and really didn't want to either.

'Lord Epacseon Darke; Epacseon is "No Escape" backwards. I know, I know, I'm a geek,' he said sheepishly and tilted his head. 'I do puzzles and I mess around with letters.' Meadow and Zade looked at each other in disbelief.

'B—but, saying that, the door is just over there,' he continued. 'I normally work on logic, but when a means of escape is dangled in front of you, well, logic goes out of the window,' Pip said, backtracking on his original statement. He looked at the door with fondness. 'Maybe we can escape and call the police and they can deal with this—this person, whatever he or whatever it is,' Pip said with hope. 'If so, then maybe they can find Tina. She could be alive and hidden away somewhere. Just because she was taken, doesn't mean she's dead.'

'You don't honestly believe that, Pip, do you?' Zade snapped. 'That is not going to be the way out and you know it. And Tina is gone, don't give me false hope.'

'It's worth a try,' he said. 'Surely?'

'I'm not leaving without Tina,' Zade retorted angrily. 'I must find her, dead or alive.'

'I'm with you, Zade,' his sister agreed.

Lord Darke's voice boomed overhead. 'One can escape; it's not impossible.'

'Uh, what do you mean, one can escape?' Zade shouted at the air. 'Where is Tina?'

Lord Darke didn't even acknowledge Zade's desperate question.

'I will allow one person to go,' he hummed. 'Which one, is up to you?' he continued calmly. His voice was condescending, smooth as silk and full of confidence. He was in charge and his boldness filled every pore of his being.

'I don't understand, we all want to go,' Meadow added shakily. 'Look, if you give us Tina back we can forget all about this, honestly,' she pleaded.

'Don't try to bargain with me.' He seemed agitated. 'I'm allowing one and only one to escape. This is my house and these are my rules. I'm giving you a chance, you stupid children.' His echo faded and, as it did so, the front door creaked open. All three of them suddenly looked in the same direction. They could easily see the drive leading up to the house; it was daylight outside, and so inviting it was almost overwhelming. There was a long whiff of cool air and mixed in was the fragrance of flowers. They could even hear birdsong somewhere. Pip rubbed his chin; his eyes were wide and he could almost touch freedom.

'Why don't we all make a run for it now?' he whispered. 'Maybe we can make it.' He was panting and licking his lips, on the verge of bursting out.

'Because he sets the rules and he's all powerful,' said Zade. 'He can hear everything we say and watch everything we do. Don't you understand yet, Pip? He's playing with us and has been all along.' Zade spoke quietly even though he knew Darke was listening. 'He has no intention of letting us go. This is all amusement to him – a game. I wouldn't trust him as far as I could throw him and we can't even find him to do that. He's not letting us go and, I'm not leaving Tina behind.'

'I don't believe him either,' Meadow confirmed. 'This could be just another trick. Anyway, we probably wouldn't even get to the door. He's messing with our heads, Pip, don't you see? Even I thought that you'd understand this guy's mind.'

'Well I don't trust him either, but I'm taking the chance,' Pip said, and with that he made a sprint for the exit. He was in full stride and ran across the open foyer.

'Pip, no! Don't!' Meadow screamed. 'Please stop, you can't trust a mad man.' As Pip approached the open door… It slammed shut! He screeched to a halt and grasped the doorknob frantically, trying to force it open. It was no use.

'Open!' he pleaded. 'Bloody open, will you!' He was breathing hard; sweat poured down his face and dripped off his chin. He stopped and then realised what he'd done. He turned slowly to face his girlfriend and her brother. Their faces were filled with burning hatred and Zade wanted to grab him but Meadow held him back.

'You would have left Meadow here without even a second thought, you filthy coward. You filthy coward,' he angrily repeated, spittle flying from his mouth. It took all of Meadow's strength just to keep him still. She wasn't that strong but pulled with all she had to keep him from killing Pip.

Zade was trembling, but not with fear, but with anger and every other damning emotion that wanted to escape his body.

'I knew you were selfish, but I didn't realise how much you valued your life above anyone else,' he said. 'The only person that should have gone was Meadow. She wouldn't go without you or me. I know that for a fact; she has courage and dignity. You have nothing.'

'No I... I,' he stuttered, realising there was no turning the clock back now. He'd shown his true colours and even despised himself. 'I... I'm sorry, Med, really I am.'

Meadow turned away, too disgusted to even look at him.

'Meadow, please, I'm sorry. I don't know what got into me. I won't ever do it again.'

But it was too late. Meadow released her grip from her brother, her arms were burning and she was panting.

'Stay away from my sister,' Zade barked, a deadly stare following the demand. 'And stay away from me if you know what's good for you.'

'Come on, Zade, calm down now,' Meadow said, soothing him as she'd done for years as a good sister does.

'Yes, yes, wonderful.' Lord Darke was laughing wildly. 'Oh my, I couldn't have wished for better. You are wonderful children.'

'He's quite mad, isn't he?' Meadow whispered to Zade as he put his arm around her in support. 'He really enjoyed us fighting, that's what all this was for,'

'Totally mad. I will find a way out, Med, trust me I will,' he said confidently. 'This guy won't be in control forever. He has to make a mistake sometime and we'll be ready.' He knew Darke could hear him. He wanted him to anyway.

Pip stayed in the background on his own and kept quiet, still despising himself for the selfish act he'd attempted.

There must be a way out of here. Zade's mind was in turmoil.

'Let's get out of here, Med,' Zade said, beginning to move away from the foyer and toward the huge double doors that stood under the balcony.

'This has got to be the ballroom or main dining area. If it is then there must be a way to get to the kitchen and out the back of the building.'

'Can I come with—' Pip asked meekly.

'No! Don't even think about it. Pip,' Zade snarled.

Meadow squeezed Zade's hand and looked unblinking into his eyes. 'Let him, please,' Meadow asked softly. 'For me, I don't want anyone left behind.'

'Don't say anything. Don't do anything,' Zade ordered.

'See, she's thinking of you even though you betrayed her.' A sharp pain of guilt stabbed at Pip's stomach. The doors opened quite easily which surprised them, especially Zade. It was like they were being led. But it wasn't a ballroom or dining room that greeted them, only another corridor.

'Damn,' Zade cursed. 'This place is driving me nuts.' He was still angry at Pip and was still reeling from the loss of his girlfriend.

The corridor was well lit with gas lamps leading the way, but the passage itself seemed to go on for miles. This place didn't match the house at all; the walls were metal. The naked flames were encased in glass intermittently lined along the sides.

'Where the hell does this go? And why metal? It doesn't even feel like we're in the house,' Zade grumbled. He reached out and touched the riveted panel. It was rusty, cold, and totally metal. He gently moved his hand towards the globe that sealed the flame inside. He could feel the heat from the glass. It was all real. He dropped his hand and peeled away a small leaf of flaking metal. He put it to his nose and sniffed. It smelled of metal decay; the earthy, tinny smell of iron. *How does he do this?* he felt himself think.

'I've seen a place like this before,' Meadow said, trying to lighten the atmosphere. He looked at her. 'It looks like the place we went through before we met you and Tina.' The name Tina brought a lump to her throat.

'This house is full of surprises,' Zade said as he squinted into the distance. All the time Pip didn't utter a word and followed obediently like a dog.

After walking for what felt like an age they could see a single door at the end.

'Another door,' Zade mumbled. Every obstacle seemed to hurt now.

'Yes, thank God,' Meadow squeaked in a dry voice. The air was suddenly filled with intermittent hissing sounds, like escaping gas. *Hiss-hiss-hiss-hiss.*

'What the heck is that?' Meadow asked, her eyes darting all around. So too were Pip and her brother's. They turned and looked behind and saw for themselves. The long rows of gaslights were gradually being extinguished in sequence. One after the other they died and gloom followed in a heavy shroud of black. It looked miles away, but the darkness was englufing, emerging like a cloak – a cloak that would eventually smother its victims.

'What's happening?' Pip spoke up. Zade ignored him but was puzzled all the same.

'It's going to be completely dark in a minute. What do we do then?' Meadow panicked.

'I don't know, maybe there's light on the other side of that door; we'll have to open it fast to find out,' said Zade. 'This is Darke's work again. There's nowhere else to go, he's setting the rules and we have to follow.' Zade looked at the door curiously; it wasn't a normal door at all. It was made of metal like the walls and there was no handle. It had a small wheel in the centre. The only time he had seen anything like it was on a submarine. He'd been on a school trip and had walked through a sub in dry dock.

His train of thought came back. 'He's pushing us to go through,' he said as it got darker. Gradually the only lights that were left on were the two either side of them. Something made Zade walk back to the darkness, a burning curiosity. He gently rubbed his right hand along the visible surface where the light was. But, as soon as his hand disappeared into the black, he jerked back in shock!

'Zade, what's wrong?' Meadow asked.

'Oh my God. There's nothing there, literally nothing there!' he answered.

'What do you mean "nothing there"?' Pip asked, but no one acknowledged him.

'Come see for yourself.' He signalled to his sister. Meadow walked to the opposite side to where Pip stood. She couldn't see anything in the blinding darkness but she did as her brother had asked and felt the wall. She felt shock course through her body; it was as he'd said, nothing but a cool rush of air. No solid surface at all. Her bottom lip trembled and she felt sick. Zade quickly knelt to the floor and reached out.

'There is literally nothing here.' He stood back and grabbed Meadow. 'The lights are going out and so is the world that exists within it.'

'But that's impossible,' Pip chirped up, running his hands along the wall. He stood there groping in the blackness. A worried look filled his already tired face. 'How can this be?'

Zade dipped his hand into his pocket and brought out a coin – a fifty pence piece. He balanced it on his thumb and index finger and flicked it into the darkness. He waited as did the other two, but nothing. There was no clank or tinkle… no sound reported at all. Zade swallowed hard.

'There is only one way to go,' he said gripping the wheel and heaving it clockwise. It didn't budge right away, but the more pressure he applied the easier it became. He turned it around and around until it clunked to a stop. The door cracked open and light beamed through.

Chapter 12

Inner Workings – Part 1

Zade pulled and felt the weight as the heavy panel opened slightly wider. He heard the sharp intake of breath from his sister and steadied himself before proceeding. Once the momentum took hold the door freely swung wide open. The full, blinding light hit them first, hurting their eyes and making them squint – and then immediately afterwards came the sound. A full cacophony of mechanical clicks, rattles, ticks, and clunks escaped from the place beyond. He was unsure whether to continue or shut it back up and retreat, but where would they go? This was the only route they could take. He gathered his courage and they walked through.

'What is it with this guy?' Zade asked. He was taken completely by surprise. All three breathed hard, the enormity of it all was overwhelming. He reasserted himself; he felt like a dot on the edge of the universe. They were standing on a precipice of a gigantic auditorium, perhaps the size of eight football pitches. Below them, stretching out on a huge scale was of all things – a clock!

'This guy is definitely obsessed with time, isn't he?' Meadow commented. 'He's a freak.' The clock was no ordinary timepiece either. The body was laid out before them, its inner workings exposed to the elements. There was an array of moving parts, all giant in size. The face itself was in the distance so you could only really appreciate it from overhead, exactly from where they were standing. From up here they could see it in all its glory. It was gigantic! It was made up of two circles forming two levels, a top level where the hour and minute hand were set, and the lower inner circle was where the second hand was seated, overhanging the outer edge. Above the face itself and built into the opposite side was what looked like another door.

Great, Zade thought, yet another stupid door to get through, he was getting tired of all this. He hated the fact that he was being controlled; he wanted to be in control of his own destiny.

'Why is everything so big?' Meadow wondered.

'And clocks?' Zade uttered. 'I used to like them, but now I hate them.'

To add to all this confusion they suddenly heard a faint scream.

'What or who was that?' Meadow quizzed, instinctively looking over to where she thought it came from.

Pip was also intrigued, but kept quiet.

The voice screeched once again and sounded familiar to Zade. For a moment, he hoped it was her but that would be impossible, he thought. He dismissed it at first, but then focused his gaze on a small moving figure on the clock face. It looked like a person, but he couldn't be sure.

'Look,' he said urgently. 'There's someone down there I think. Whoever it is, must be in trouble... or another trap!'

'I can't see, is it a boy or girl?' Meadow asked.

'I... I'm... not sure.' Zade lifted his right hand to shade his eyes from the lights. 'I... It looks like, no it can't be... Tina,' he said in total astonishment.

Pip leaned forward and saw it was, in fact, Tina. 'It is, I'm sure of it,' Pip mumbled, but Zade didn't acknowledge his inclusion into the conversation and just gave him a sharp look of disgust. A look that warned him to stay out of the way.

'Oh my God, sh—she's alive. Zade, she's alive!' Meadow screeched excitedly, starting to jump up and down on the spot. 'What's she doing there? She looks as if she's been tied up.'

'B—but that's impossible, it can't be her, sh—she drowned.' Zade couldn't believe it. Is this an evil trick, or is she actually still alive? He was almost tearful. 'Tina! *Tina!*' he shouted frantically, but she couldn't hear him. *Why is she screaming?* he wondered. He couldn't work it out from here. 'If she's in pain, I'll kill him if he's hurt her.' The thoughts were whirring around in his head. *What danger is she in?* He couldn't think straight. One moment he'd been grieving her death and now she's... alive! His heart was racing with an excitement that you could only associate with Christmas, the excitement of something unexpected.

'That minute hand looks awfully close to her body, Zade,' said Meadow. 'When it comes around next time...'

'That must be why she's screaming. He's going to kill her for real this time, for his amusement.' Zade was adamant that he wasn't going to let her be harmed again. *This ends now*, he thought; the determination was fixed in his mind. 'You're right, Med, that arm is too close to her.' He stopped; he couldn't bring himself to continue.

'It will cut her in half,' Pip interrupted, unblinking.

'Yeah, thanks for that,' said Zade, giving Pip a seething glare. 'I'm not going to let that happen. The time on that clock is quarter past three, so we've got an hour to get to her before it does. Me and Tina have already been through this type of thing before,' Zade added. 'This Darke guy is obsessed with clocks and timers and we are his guinea pigs,' he pondered for a moment. 'Probably, once he's killed us off then he'll get some other poor sods to continue his game. But I'm going to prove him wrong.'

'But he didn't kill her, Zade,' Meadow said trembling, 'so maybe we are going to be here forever.' The realisation made her bite back the tears. 'I don't want to be here forever,' she said fearfully.

'I don't understand what's happening here. Sooner or later we're not going to make it in time and someone is really going to get killed,' Zade surmised. 'We can't keep this up forever. So, once we've gone, he'll have to get some other unsuspecting kids to play his little game. So, to stop that happening, we are going to beat him. No one else is going to have to endure this nightmare.'

'How are we going to get through there in time to save her?' Pip asked, looking at the pathways to the clock face. It was like a city of cog-shaped buildings and movable roads. 'We aren't going to make it. We'll just get killed by trying to rescue her,' he said bluntly.

'Yeah, that's right leave her to die. It's what you do, isn't it?' Zade spat. 'Don't you ever think of anyone bar yourself? I've had just about enough of you Pip. Firstly, you left my sister for your own safety and now, you're thinking of yourself again and leaving Tina. Well you can stay here and rot for all I care. You've shown us your true colours, buddy. You are a coward and I'm this close to knocking your head off.'

'I don't have to listen to you and I'm no coward,' Pip countered defiantly, half-stepping toward Zade, but Zade was having none of it. All the anger and frustration came out in one right-fisted blow. He hit Pip smack in the face and sent him reeling to the floor. It was no contest. Zade was fit and lean, Pip was not a fighter. He raised his fist again and Meadow screamed from behind. He realised the situation.

'No more, Zade, he's had enough.'

He came to his senses and stopped. All the frustration and anger had released itself. He relaxed his fists and calmed down. Soon a bruise and swelling appeared on Pip's cheek and he touched it tenderly and winced. Meadow didn't try to intervene any more, but also felt no satisfaction. But she understood why her brother had done what he did. She didn't condone violence but knew her brother was only protecting her. She peered down at her ex-boyfriend.

'I don't know why I ever went out with you in the first place,' she said, filled with bitterness. 'Zade is right, you don't care about anybody but yourself. I thought I knew you, but obviously I don't.'

He tried to speak in his defence, but nothing would come.

Pip peered back at her sheepishly. She turned away and faced her brother; he was rubbing his knuckles, reddened by the blow.

'Come on, Med, the clock is ticking – literally. We haven't time for this crap.'

Zade grasped her hand and led her away. She was trembling and so was he. He reasserted himself and set his mind to the task ahead.

'Right,' he said, and she could tell that he was trying to work out which way to proceed. Zade's mind was working overtime. *Where, where, should I go?* It was a mechanical nightmare. So many avenues lay ahead.

There were steps leading down to the mechanism but he was reluctant to go the simple way. Their host was obviously watching every move and had traps set out everywhere. But Zade honestly couldn't see any other way, so that's where they had to proceed.

'We can't leave him,' Meadow whispered, still feeling guilty even after all he'd all he'd done to betray her.

'Yes we can,' Zade replied with a grimace.

Pip didn't follow anyway, he sat sulking on the steps and neither Meadow nor Zade turned back to look. The first thing they came across was a large, flat, horizontal cog that didn't seem to be moving at all. There was plenty of width to walk along so they stepped on.

'I—It feels like some kind of theme park ride,' Meadow explained, trying to smile and make light of their situation.

'Well, at least there are no queues. Remember Thorpe Park? And we don't have to pay.' They moved on with no confidence in their endeavours. Beyond the huge cog was a multitude of dangers that had to be dealt with. Zade swallowed hard and looked for the best possible path.

'God, this thing is like a minefield. Just stay close, Med, and we'll try and take an easier route,' said Zade. They shimmied along the base and came to a three-cog set-up. Each one was on top of the other like coins, a large one at the bottom and gradually getting smaller as it got to the top. It looked simple to step up, but from here on in, the parts were big and moving in different sequences. It was difficult to take in all the different movements. The whole thing was in perfect symmetry. Everything seemed sharp and dangerous and could easily snag their clothes and pull them in like a pack of mechanical wolves waiting for their next meal.

The siblings came to a narrow section and Zade swivelled his body at an angle to get through. It looked easy enough but he was still cautious. He slowly shuffled his way in but the leg of his jeans got caught between two interweaving parts. Suddenly, and without really doing anything wrong, he couldn't move. He immediately realised that he was in danger and something tight squeezed his chest. He swallowed hard and then – gently at first, without panicking – began tugging to set himself free. It was no use; the material of his jeans was stuck. He realised quickly the danger he was in and furiously tugged at his leg. The clockwork motion was slowly dragging him into the machine.

'Jesus,' he whispered to himself, 'how did this happen? I'm supposed to be the one who's switched on.'

'Oh my God, Zade!' Meadow shouted, frantically trying to pull him out. She was panicking, her face etched with sheer horror.

'Zade—Zade, oh my God, oh my God,' she repeated hysterically, tugging hard at his waistband. But it was no use; he continued to be sucked towards a revolving shaft with a slim disk-like coin above it. He was lucky that the speed was slow, giving him at least a little bit of time to think. He realised that unless he pulled himself free it would slice straight through him and the cogs would chew him up and swallow his remains inside the mechnism. This was not good. The more it pulled him in the less movement he had to free himself. The cogs clunked and clunked and tugged at his leg until he was half a metre or so away from the blade. He had to come up with something fast, but there were no options left. So, he decided there and then to accept it.

'Leave me, Med. Go on, get away from here,' he growled, knowing there wasn't much time and not wanting his sister to see this. 'You can't help me, just get away from here.'

'No! No! I'm not leaving you. Pip! Pip! Help us, please help us!' she screamed, crying and pulling at his belt, trying her hardest to free him. Zade didn't really want Pip to come but he was in no position to refuse. Meadow was still tugging and screaming uncontrollably when Zade felt his jeans rip and the sensation of being dragged backwards away from danger. In a matter of seconds he was free!

He sat down, panting and sweating, his face red with the struggle. Finally, he looked up to meet Pip and the bruise he'd given him on his left cheek. Zade closed his eyes and clenched his teeth.

'Thanks,' he said, though it hurt him to say it. He opened his eyes again and nodded respectfully. Meadow threw her arms around her brother and was inconsolable for a time.

'We started this journey together and we'll finish it together,' Pip said. 'Sorry, Meadow, I was stupid and cowardly, I'm really, really sorry. I'll understand if you don't want to talk to me any more. But we all have to stick together now, especially after this; anything could happen,' he seemed like a different person from then; there was real regret in those brown eyes.

'What's done is done, Pip. We have to help Tina now and get out of here,' Meadow replied. 'You two have to make up, there's no other way.'

'There's not much time, we have to go,' Zade said as he got to his feet.

'Do you want to take a few more minutes?' Pip asked, trying to mend the broken friendship.

'Minutes are what we don't have,' Zade explained, ignoring the gesture. 'This monster, Lord Darke, is really twisted. We are up against the clock and that's the way he likes to play it. I don't know if we can make it, but we have to try.' He quickly peered around, looking for a way through. 'Now, I really don't know which path to take; it's a maze. We have to go with our instincts.'

Once more, as a tight nit group, they continued on.

Chapter 13

Inner Workings – Part 2

'Let's go this way,' Pip said, pointing towards another area that led down a slope and away from a complex section of moving parts. The slope itself was a wide metal path that bounced when they walked on it. The air was filled with the smell of oil; obviously the special fluid needed to grease the working parts of the clock.

'Take it easy here,' Pip said with caution. 'It's like a trampoline.'

At the bottom, there was a huge wheel with four spokes protruding from a centre spindle.

'I'm sure this part turns at a far slower rate than any of the others,' Pip assumed as he tried to figure out the mechanism. 'It may be safer to cross here.'

Meadow was more concentrating than listening, trying to keep her balance.

'How do you know all this stuff?' Zade enquired, finally getting around to talking to him properly.

Pip all of a sudden, felt a small bond with Zade. 'I don't know,' he said shaking his head. 'You pick things up from time to time I suppose. I like gadgets and clockwork stuff, boring really,' he admitted.

They balanced along the flimsy, springy arm and came to a stop. Each of them listened to the sounds that were playing out above their heads. It was actually amazing to hear. Clocks tick – Zade knew that, but when you're so close to the inner workings, you can also hear every other part doing its thing. He was impressed. *Never thought I would actually be inside a clock to appreciate it*, he thought, not wanting to appear a nerd.

'Oh, wow,' Pip said, sounding surprised but worried. He stopped to linger for a moment, looking intently at something. He seemed a little excited.

'What's the matter?' Meadow asked, still a little freaked out.

'There – look.' He pointed with concern to a gap in the metal. For the first time they realised what was actually underneath the clock workings… nothing! The clock itself was suspended in mid-air. The light which lit up this huge room didn't seem to have a source either, but it did show the vastness of the drop. In fact, when they thought about it, all the light they'd seen so far didn't seem to be coming from anywhere. Zade, Pip, and Meadow stood breathless.

'How is all this possible?' Zade questioned out loud. He was annoyed. 'A clock suspended in a huge cavern full of artificial light, steps that lead nowhere, a floor that turns into quicksand and then back again into a solid floor? And my girlfriend, who had drowned and scared the life out of me, coming back to life? This guy has a lot to answer for. He can't be human.'

'These are questions we have to think about later,' Pip said. 'For now we have to get across this gap to there.' He showed them the other side by pointing it all out. 'Time is against us,' he said ominously.

'How are we supposed to get to the other side?' Meadow asked with a gulp.

'There.' Pip remarked, raising his index finger. Meadow gulped again and her eyes widened.

Above them were three interlinking horizontal cogs. They resembled fifty pence coins, only bronze instead of silver. The first one turned anti-clockwise, the second smaller one spun clockwise, and the last one again anti-clockwise. The whole apparatus was moving click by click.

'What on earth do you expect us to do?' Meadow quizzed, not wanting to know the answer.

'Well,' Zade cut in before Pip could react, 'I expect we'll have to grab a tooth and hold on until we can reach the other end. But we'll have to let go in between, because we'll get our hands mashed in that other cog. Simple, really.'

Meadow examined the movement more closely. If she didn't get this right...

She paused and looked at where the teeth interwove. This was the most frightening so far. She felt sick to her stomach and swallowed hard.

'Did I mention that I'm hating clocks more and more?' she said with a nervous puff.

'There is literally no other way around, Med.' Pip said, shaking his head in submission. 'It looks harder than it is,' he continued confidently. 'Really'

'Who's going first?' she asked, shooting a glare at both of them.

'I'll go,' Pip insisted, stepping forward. 'If it doesn't work, then you'll have to find another way.'

Zade was moved by this act of sacrifice and patted him on the shoulder, but said nothing. Pip nodded in compliance and stepped up onto a bracket. He grasped at the nearest cog and held on, a nervous feeling gripped his stomach.

'Please work, please work,' he mumbled to himself, his heart racing at a furious pace. He wasn't used to physical activities only, brainwork. He couldn't let Meadow and Zade down this time though. He had to prove himself.

It took about twenty clicks to get right over to the other side and did actually look easy enough. Even the interchanges looked pretty simple. He gave them the thumbs up when he landed and let out a huge gasp of nervous air.

'Right, Med, you go next,' Zade said, gesturing with both hands in a sweeping motion.

'Uh-uh. Maybe you should go first,' she stammered. 'Just to give me another look at how it's done.' Zade looked at her with reluctance.

'Med, come on, you're good at gymnastics, miles better than me. This should be a piece of cake for you.' He looked at her with wide eyes and playfully nudged her shoulder.

'Yeah, but that was with a net underneath me. There's no net and there's no bottom. Jesus.' She realised the predicament they were all in. 'Also, I don't like moving parts; they make me nervous.'

'And there's also no way back and Tina is going to die,' Zade added, getting angry with her.

'OK, OK.' She knew what he was like when he became angry – impossible to argue with – and so climbed up and concentrated. She stood and paced herself, it felt like one of those games on telly. A game with a deadly timer and instead of a huge prize at the end it may be the loss of her friend. After a few seconds the cogs became mesmerising. The sound they made was overwhelming. She began to breathe hard and felt faint. 'You can't do this, Med, you can't,' she told herself.

'Grab it, Med.' Pip shouted from the other end. His voice jumbled her thoughts. This jolted her back into reality.

'OK, I'm ready,' she said, grabbing hold of the nearest cog. It was cold and her hands were sweaty. She hesitated but the movement of the wheel was relentless and pulled at her fingers and arms. It tugged her out into the open and she hung loosely, like a thread of cotton. But the second click made her lose grip and one hand released. Both Pip and Zade realised she was in trouble. But Zade couldn't grab her or she would definitely fall. He quickly clambered up onto the bracket and gripped on behind her. By the time he was moving, Meadow was frantically hanging on by her fingertips!

'Help! Help!' she cried. She was swaying back and forth like a pendulum. She could feel tears welling up in her eyes. 'Oh God, oh God.'

'Med, stay calm and don't look down,' Zade said, only a few metres behind. 'I'm right behind you, don't worry,' he called out, but as soon as he'd mentioned not looking down that was the first thing she did and she screamed.

'I... I can't hold on,' she sobbed. 'I'm going to fall. I'm going to die.'

'No you're not. You can do this, Meadow Long. Listen to me.' But his persuasion wasn't working so he had to guide her the best that he could. 'You have to swap cogs in a second,' Zade insisted.

'You're not Mum, Zade,' she said defiantly. Zade looked down as Pip looked on helplessly. He swallowed hard.

'Just keep holding on, it's not far away now, we're almost there. But you have to lift your left hand and grab the bigger cog, Med,' he said with a deep-seated terror in the pit of his throat.

'That's it, Med, you can do it,' said Pip. Words of encouragement were coming from him on the other side too.

The cog clunked on and Meadow looked down.

'Grab the cog with your other hand, Med… *now!*' Zade screamed.

Meadow let out a grunt before swinging her free arm and gripping the bigger cog on the other side.

'Let go, Med. Let go quickly with your other hand,' said Zade, terrified. Meadow realised her predicament and finally let go and was again hanging in mid-air. Zade almost forgot himself as he concentrated on his sister. He nearly got jammed in the intertwining cogs too. He only had a matter of seconds before he would be mashed up in the same motion. He flicked himself over just in time and swung limply behind her.

'Don't look down, Med, look towards your idiot of a boyfriend,' he said, almost out of breath.

Meadow continued, not knowing what had just happened in her wake.

'I—I can't hold on any longer,' she screamed, before slipping off.

'No! Meadow!' Zade cried out, but he couldn't do anything to stop her from falling.

Pip reached out and managed to grab her arm and somehow wrenched her into his arms. She yelped and couldn't say anything. Zade jumped off and landed next to the pair of them. He finally collapsed onto the platform.

'Are you all right?' he asked.

She nodded vigorously, not having the breath to talk quite yet.

Moments passed and they knew that they didn't have time to stay and take a break, they had to continue. Tina needed them.

'Come on, you two, we have to go.' Pip urged. She blinked pursed her lips, shaking her head in acknowledgement.

'Look, there's an upright bracket that we can climb and take us up to the next level,' Pip said he was already working his way forward. 'Quickly, come on.'

'I'm not climbing on another moving cog again,' Meadow said adamantly.

'It's not moving, Med, it's just a wide metal arm,' said Pip. 'You can do this. You climbed up that door easily.' He smiled with his usual grin that melted her.

'OK, let's go,' Zade interrupted as they moved on and saw that they were in fact not far away from the clock face now. They could actually see Tina and she could see them, but alarmingly the minute hand was just coming off twelve. Zade's eyes bulged.

'Jesus, we've only got about a quarter of an hour,' Zade realised. 'We can't let her down now. We're almost there.'

'It does look straightforward from here though, Zade,' Pip added, not wanting to sound too confident. 'We should make it to her in plenty of time, don't worry.' He squeezed his arm. 'I'm here to help this time.'

Suddenly, a loud rattling in the distance grabbed their attention. It sounded like an anchor being released on a ship.

'What on earth's happening now?' Meadow asked. 'I can't cope with much more.' Her nerves were frazzled by this point. In the next few moments they were speechless. From the position they'd entered into the arena, a platform was being lowered. This platform was connected by a series of chains. From below it looked like a huge metal rectangular cage. They looked on in curiosity and bewilderment.

'What's in there and why is it here?' Pip mouthed.

'I don't know, but it doesn't look good,' Zade countered, just as mystified. By the time it came into view, they could see that the platform was occupied. But what with?

'Who are they?' Meadow asked. The cage was only metres away from the floor. It came to a halt and grounded with a huge clang. Then there was silence. The gate dropped open and another humongous bang ensued. Then, with military precision, out stepped what could only be described as a unit of soldiers. They actually emerged out of the cage in sequence and looked like metal men!

'Jesus, that mad fool must have sent them to get us. They look like robots,' Pip said weakly, both fascinated and scared out of his wits at the same time. The figures stood perfectly still in a row, their body armour gleaming under the lights. From where the teenagers were standing they could just make out the mechanised parts that made up the automatons.

Each one stood at about six feet tall. They didn't appear to be carrying weapons, maybe they didn't need them, Pip thought. But how could they be working without electrical energy? Darke is a maniac, but he's also a genius if he can make something run endlessly on a clockwork mechanism.

'Good grief, how many are there?' Zade waited for them all to disembark.

'F—Four,' Meadow said, stammering as she counted.

'Four too many,' Pip gasped, 'we've got two problems now, saving Tina and keeping out of their way.'

The soldiers, once assembled, began their pursuit and that shocked the young crew into action. The automated platoon of soldiers moved with precision into the clockwork city and the teenagers turned and fled.

'Let's get out of here!' Zade barked. 'Come on, quickly.'

'There's only this long bar to get over. Then climb over that shaft with the spring and along that other piece of metal,' Pip explained. 'That will take us to the metal girder that holds the hands to the clock,'

They all moved off and were at the bottom of the clock face in no time. As luck would have it the two circles that held the numbers were fixed together by fancy metal brackets that could be used as a ladder.

'Well that was easier for a change, up here quickly,' Pip shouted through the confusion. On the clock there were five minutes left before the minute hand would do its damage. The three of them were now on the hour arm. Tina couldn't see them at first and was calling out in distress.

'Tina, we're here, don't worry,' Zade called out.

She saw him up close for the first time since she'd been swallowed up by the ground. A huge sense of relief and warmth and hope filled her.

'Zade—Zade, thank God you're all right,' she sobbed.

Thank God I'm all right, he thought, she's always thinking of others first.

'I'm fine,' he said tearfully as he tugged at her ropes. He was more excited than he'd ever felt in his life. The other two soon came to his aid and Tina gave them a big smile. It took a bit of doing but the ropes eventually gave way. They got her out of danger with only two minutes to go, before the arm was about to cut overhead. She was finally reunited with her friends again and tears streamed down her soft white cheeks. He hugged her for all he was worth. She didn't say anything, just hugged him back.

'I'm never letting you go again,' he promised, almost squeezing the life out of her. 'Never.'

'I'm not going to go off any more on my own either. You... you can let me breathe now, Zade,' she said, wrestling her way out of the bear hug. She rubbed her wrists and ankles, sore from the tethers.

'Zade, sorry, but we haven't time for this now,' Pip interrupted. 'Those soldiers are getting closer, they're coming and we have to go,' he said urgently.

Zade had forgotten all about the imminent danger they were in. He was too tangled up in seeing his girlfriend alive again to think of anything else. But they were all in danger and they had to go.

'Zade, Pip's right we have to go,' Meadow said. She sounded insistent. 'Look, they're coming down there.'

'What's going on?' Tina cut in, not up to speed on the clockwork enemy.

'There—' Zade pointed in the distance to the advancing soldiers. 'We're being followed by those and we have to go. Darke is still setting the rules and it's getting more dangerous for us, they're gaining.' They all ran across the circle of numbers and leapt over the hour hand. It was a lot easier than trying to dodge springs and cogs. This was in the open and speed was of the essence. Soon they were all off the face of the clock and heading upwards. The doorway they saw from the other side was now in front of them.

'We have to go this way.' Pip pushed it open and revealed yet another long corridor. All of them had a sinking feeling inside. The feeling of eventual doom.

'Where the hell does this one lead?' Meadow cursed. 'I can't take much more of this.' But when she looked behind her and saw how close the soldiers were, it changed her mind.

'There is again no other way to go. Med, we have to go this way,' Pip said.

'Whatever we're going to do, I think we'd better hurry,' Tina said as they all took a quick glance behind. They saw that the clockwork robots were already halfway along the mechanism. Negotiating the tangle of moving parts as if they weren't there. They were relentless and marched forward a lot quicker than they had.

'Oh God, why do they want us?' Tina said, her cracked voice piercing the air.

'Lord Darke again. He's mental and not about to change soon,' Zade said, not even looking at his friends. He was staring into space.

'Let's go quickly, they'll be here soon,' Pip shrieked. 'Come on, or they'll catch us.'

All four disappeared into the tunnel. The sound of the clock eventually diminished, but the sound of stamping metal feet became louder.

Chapter 14

Clockwork Robots

They ran deep into the heart of the tunnel, the fear of being caught urging them on. Finally, the passageway opened out into a vast network of metal platforms and stairways that seemed so familiar. They all stopped to catch their breath.

'This is just like the clock tower but bigger,' Pip panted. 'It just gets boring looking at the same scene after a while.' Everything rolled on endlessly, giving them each a depressing feeling in the pits of their stomach.

'How long can we keep this up?' Meadow gasped breathlessly. 'I don't think I can go much further; they're bound to catch us eventually.'

'I'm with you, Meadow,' Tina gasped. 'I don't know how long I can go either. But then again.' She took another breath. 'I'd never sunk into a pool of liquid tiles... and survived before... either.' She gulped and continued. 'Or had robots chasing me.' She couldn't talk anymore and bent over gasping, her legs felt like rubber.

'I can hear them, they're no far away,' Zade said, puffing with urgency. 'We have to keep going – now stop talking and just run.' Behind them was the ominous *stomp-stomp-stomp* of the mechanical marching soldiers. They didn't sound as they though were tiring at all, not like the four escaping youngsters.

'Where shall we go?' Pip said, looking blankly at the many routes they could take. 'We should split up, that cuts the enemy down to two each. We have more chance fighting off two than four at once,' he calculated.

'Two—four, it doesn't really matter, does it?' Zade said. 'We can't stop any of them. We don't have any weapons and besides, they're armoured. What do we have to defend ourselves?' Zade was right in his answer, and quickly responded. 'But we all stick together this time. No splitting up. I'm not losing anyone again.'

The heavy metallic sound of clanking footsteps descending the first set of stairs echoed into the abyss. The steel structure groaned under the immense pressure. They could feel the vibration through the metal grid underfoot. The four teenagers moved across a long platform until it ended in a three-way exit, and stopped! There were steps leading up to the right, steps directly ahead that led down to the lower levels, and another metal corridor to their left. They looked at one another and shrugged their shoulders.

'Does it really matter which way we go?' Tina questioned.. 'Up, down, left, right; it all seems pointless anyway.'

'We can't give up, Teen. Now come on,' Zade snapped.

A loud and calamitous stomping filled the air, making their minds up for them. The teenagers knew that the metal men were right behind them. Zade pointed a finger ahead and they all agreed to go forward and down. Exhausted, and with aching bodies, they pushed on, each one tired of running. This new route led to a long open bridge that could only be attacked in single file.

The bridge itself consisted of long tubular handrails to each side, with intermittent struts dropping from the rails and connecting to the base. The floor was a metre-wide metal lattice that stretched all the way along the length, from one end to the other. Besides the handrails and posts every couple of metres there was nothing else to stop anyone falling off. In true leadership fashion Zade went first, followed by Meadow, Tina and Pip bringing up the rear.

'Grab hold of the handrail; as you can see, it's a long way down and there's not much between us and that.' Zade informed them ominously pointing to the open space below.

Pip anxiously waited in line and peered over his shoulder, hoping the enemy wasn't that close yet. If they were, he would be the one to take the brunt of it. He couldn't get past anyone and it scared him, but he wasn't going to be a coward anymore. The girls always come first now, this thought made him feel stronger inside.

They ran to the other end, making the framework sway slightly under the weight of their footsteps. The sound of their feet slapping against the catwalk gave away their position and they cursed themselves for it. Zade saw there was another network of steel in front, just like the one they'd left behind. Another maze of metal.

'Good grief,' he said, shutting his eyes in frustration and thought, *Where the hell do we go from here?*

When they gathered on the other side of the bridge, Pip spoke up. 'Zade, look, this is a great place for an ambush.

Look, there are places on both sides here—' He pointed excitedly upwards to two points of attack. 'We can try and stop them, you know, push them off somehow. It's an idea.'

Zade took in what he was saying and surveyed the immediate area.

'They can only come over in single file like us. It's a perfect opportunity to try and finish this,' Pip said. 'What do you think?'

'You're right, Pip. Maybe we can stop them and turn things around. It's worth a try anyway. Good one, pal,' he said in agreement. 'We need some kind of weapon though, to attack them with.' Zade looked around, searching for something heavy, something he could handle and use as a club. He saw what he was looking for and smiled. One of the handrails at the top of the steps, to his right, was open ended. He ran up and quickly worked it back and forth until it gave in and snapped off. He felt the weight of it in his hand and a smile broadened his face.

He grabbed one end firmly with both hands. He swung out in a few sweeping motions, like a baseball bat, until he felt comfortable. That'll do, he told himself.

Pip saw what he was doing and did the same on the other side. It took him a little longer to break it off but they now both had metal bars they could use as makeshift clubs.

'At least we're armed now,' Zade said with satisfaction and Pip agreed. This made the girls uneasy, seeing the warrior look in their partners' eyes; it felt like a scene from *Lord of the Flies*.

'I don't like this, Zade,' Tina said shakily. 'I hate violence.'

'Me neither,' Meadow agreed, feeling scared at the hate that Pip had manifested.

'Look, it's either us or them. We really have no choice in this now. If we don't defend ourselves then they will kill us,' Zade said with conviction, but he looked different now, not the teenage boy Tina had been dating, but a man. 'Honestly, I don't like this either, but we have you two to defend and ourselves.'

'Med, there's no other way,' Pip added. 'If they intend to kill us then I'd rather go down fighting. I've never felt this way before, but I feel I need to protect you and not run away this time.' This struck a chord in Meadow's heart and she stepped forward and kissed him full on the lips.

'Right, what are we supposed to do?' Meadow asked with Tina by her side. 'We can fight too, you know,' she responded before looking at Tina. 'I don't like violence either, Teen, but the boys are right; it's them or us.'

'No—No, you two keep on running down there until we can catch up,' Zade said adamantly, ominously pointing into the distance. 'It's far too dangerous and I don't want any of you to get hurt.' He was pushing Meadow, shoving her and Tina away.

'No, no way,' Tina snapped angrily. 'I'm not going anywhere. You said it yourself, no splitting up this time, and we're not, Zade. We're not!' She was determined and he could see that there was no chance of changing either of their minds.

'That's right, Teen, he did say that,' Meadow cut in. 'Anyway, seriously, we can help.'

'Med—' Pip was about to argue, but when she looked at him he shook his head and said nothing. He knew she was so strong-willed that there was no budging her.

'OK, OK. You can stay, but you have to hide over there. I'm not putting you in any danger,' said Zade. 'There's also nothing else we can use for weapons, so you have to hide.' That did make sense and the girls responded with a nod of compliance.

The bridge suddenly started to vibrate and the echoed clank of steel against steel broke their debate.

'Go quickly before they see you,' Zade said. He immediately turned to Pip and breathed. 'All right, they're here. Pip, do you know what we have to do?' Zade said.

'We haven't had time to devise a plan yet, have we?' Pip said in haste. Zade thought for a second.

'Here's the plan. As soon as they get close, we step out from hiding up there and smash the hell into them.'

'OK.' Pip gulped with excitement and fear and everything else that was bouncing around in his head. His hands were already sweaty, grasping the cold metal shaft. His legs felt like jelly; he'd never done anything like this before. He wasn't going to run away this time, he kept telling himself. When he saw them in the distance, advancing across the first part of the bridge, he wanted to run. But the horrible feeling he'd felt when he'd left them the last time came flooding back. This gave him strength. Not this time!

The girls moved behind the stairwell and crouched out of sight, holding each other tight. The boys hid on the stairs above the bridge, concealed by a criss-cross of metalwork.

Zade was taking quick shallow breaths, coolly concentrating, while Pip was panting like a puppy and sweating like a pig. Sure enough, there was only room for each mechanical man to negotiate the bridge in single-file. A wry smile of satisfaction filtered across the two boys' faces. This part of the plan was falling into place.

The soldiers entered one by one and trudged across, shaking the foundations as they marched. Each of the boys were tense – ready and waiting to pounce. The vibrations through the metal made it almost impossible for them to concentrate. Zade looked over to Pip, shook his head, and mouthed "Not yet". Pip understood, but his heart was beating so fast he thought he was going to pass out. The pounding of feet on the bridge felt as though the enemy was closer than they actually were. Pip swallowed hard, holding down the bile in his throat. Zade, although the more assertive of the two, still had the butterflies bouncing around in the pit of his stomach.

The enemy had passed the halfway mark and Zade's grip on his weapon grew tighter, almost to the point of strangulation. Pip too was gripping his club so tight that he could barely feel his hands. Both their hearts now were beating faster than a runaway train. Adrenaline pumping through their veins, they felt the urge to scream out in frustration, but they kept cool heads. *Come on, come on,* thought Zade. His mind was working overtime. He was sweating, making his hands clammy. His fringe was damp and droplets trickled into his eyes.

'You can do this, you can do this,' Zade whispered, convincing himself over and over. If they could have heard each other's thoughts they would have been shocked by just how scared they both were. Zade looked at Pip and showed three fingers on his left hand in a countdown. He then dropped it down to two, and then one. This was it, no more pretending, they were here! Without thinking, and only the adrenalin leading, they surged forward.

Both warriors leapt off the stairs, shouting and screaming their battle cry and rushed at the first unsuspecting figure. Pip quickly lashed out with his bar and, to his utter surprise, knocked its head completely off with the first blow.

Zade's effort smashed into the side of the bodywork and it buckled under the impact. They connected on two more hits, one each; and the first soldier bent double and fell off the bridge and into oblivion.

'Pip, move,' Zade screamed. They didn't have time to savour their victory as the second one came at them. Zade this time sent a blow to its right arm and, with the force, the arm snapped clean off. But to their amazement it did not slow it down in the slightest; it still surged forward. Pip was ready for it though and let go a volley of blows to its head and side like a manic Bruce Lee.

'Come and get me, you useless hunk of metal,' Pip bellowed as he and Zade kept on until it crumpled under the reign of blows and fell to the floor. Zade looked at Pip with a sense of mystery, this guy was enjoying this battle a little too much, he thought. But they were distracted with all their efforts focused on number two. They didn't see number three coming at them. For the first time they were taken by surprise and the game had changed.

It gripped Pip by the arm and was trying to throw him over the side. He clumsily dropped his weapon and just about managed to hold onto the handrail.

'Help me, Zade, he's got my arm.' Pip's agitated voice caught his comrade's attention.

Zade flew into action and tried to smash the clockwork androids legs from under it. Refocused on its new foe, the automaton disregarded its grip on Pip. Its right hand grabbed the bar that Zade was holding. Pip took his chance and pulled away and pushed with all his might. Zade did the same, not letting go of his metal bar, but also pushing hard. With double the effort, they forced it over the edge and watched it fall. It looked as though it was still trying to climb back up as it got smaller and smaller. There was nothing to grip onto and so it was swallowed up by the dark.

Clockwork man number two was still squirming on the bridge. It was trying to get back up and was on its feet but it couldn't straighten up. Pip took initiative, rushed forward and gripped it under the gusset.

'Come on, Zade, help me quickly. Before it has time to attack.'

Zade followed suit and they hoisted the ailing robot over the side. It tried to fight them off with its remaining limb but the youngsters were having none of it. With one more surge of energy they pushed it over with the others. They yelped and whooped in victory and the grins on their faces told the story. They blew a huge sigh of relief at a job well done, but then remembered there was still one more of the clockwork soldiers left to fight.

'Quickly, come on. One to go,' Zade said as they spun around to face the last one. Pip was spent but he knew he had to carry on. They were both drained but when they looked the last soldier wasn't there.

'Oh my God,' Pip squeaked. 'Where has it gone?'

'Oh my God,' was all Zade could utter.

Chapter 15

Loose Cannon

Pip and Zade quickly turned when they heard screams from the girls. There it was – the fourth clockwork robot, large as life and heading straight for them. Zade was still trying to work out how the mechanical man got past him, without either he or Pip noticing. Pip, though, was already on a mission. He'd got ahead of Zade and quickly tried to grab the metal monster in some kind of hold. Unfortunately for him, he had no way to defend himself. He was no match for its automatic strength and agility.

The robot turned and lashed out, his right hand caught Pip on his left shoulder, which spun him around like a spinning top. He went spiralling to the floor, not really registering what had just happened. He lay dazed, stars dancing before his eyes. The robot refocused its mission and made for the defenceless teenager.. It was about to grab Pip when the girls screamed hysterically, distracting it again. This alerted its focus to their position, so it turned around and once again headed straight for them.. That was Zade's chance and he didn't waste any time. He lunged at his enemy, hoping to grasp around its neck, or arms, or anything really. But his super-quick plan didn't quite work out.

He was looking to smash its head into the framework somehow, but tripped at the last second. He only managed to impact its left side in a sort of half rugby tackle. It did the trick though, and the unit toppled over onto its side.

Zade was amazed and swiftly got to his feet and surged forward again. He grabbed the robot's left arm as it tried to grip the handrail to right itself. It was a powerful limb and he held on for all he could. He waited with squinted eyes and tensed his body for the impact of its right arm, but nothing happened. He then realised it was jammed underneath its torso. Zade couldn't believe his luck. With a quick flick of his body he sat on the robots clockwork frame in a wrestler's grip; scissoring his legs around the shoulder area. He pulled and pulled back as hard he could, it felt like a giant joystick. Close up, he could see the detail involved in the make-up of the being. Its arm was a series of rods and wires and intricate cogs and spindles encased in a mesh of metal skin. Its hand looked much like that of a human and the fingers wriggled in much the same way. Lord Darke was a clever engineer as well as a maniac.

Zade wrenched back again on its arm and was a lot more successful. He heard a creak and then a snap and finally managed to break off the robots left limb completely. He fell onto his back and for a moment tried to compose himself, ready for the next bout.

He looked on and saw the android was thrashing around trying to right itself with its one remaining arm. Zade stood up and reached down, grasping the severed limb that was lying by the ailing robot's side. He lifted it, like a club and was just about to slam it down on the creature's head. Unfortunately for him, the robot had flipped over and was now on its back. It saw Zade wielding the weapon and so grabbed it in mid-air with its remaining hand, stopping him in his tracks. The two wrestled like gladiators and, in the struggle, the limb slipped free and was lost over the side.

Instinctively the robot gripped Zade's collar, and pulled him down towards its face. Zade used both hands to try and free himself, but couldn't. It was a surreal moment; he was face to face with something that was moving but its features were as dead as death itself.

He could hear the grinding of gears from within, they seemed to moan and complain almost like a voice. He couldn't take his eyes off the facial features either; it was weird. It had sockets for eyes and a slot for a mouth, all superficial and only for show. It also had small slots on each side of its head, probably a hearing mechanism. Zade spoke into the earpiece.

'Listen, Darke, you won't stop us from leaving,' he whispered through gritted teeth, spittle leaking into the ear. 'You won't beat us. Give it up now.' But there was no response and, the robot still had him. He had to break free and get away.

'Let go, you git. Let me go.' He squirmed and struggled. He could smell the oil and fumes resonating from within. It was obviously burning out from a part of the mechanism. As he wrestled, his belt buckle got caught in the machinery by its belly. It was an open interface and so the metal edge jammed and stopped some of its movement. The groan from the cogs and spindles slowed the robot's persistence, and it released its grip fractionally, enough for Zade to pull away. He quickly got to his feet as the buckle pulled out.

'Quick, run! Run, you idiots,' Zade ranted. 'Come on, Pip, help push this thing over the edge.'

Pip got to his feet and the girls moved out into the open. Zade was stamping and kicking like someone possessed and the metal man was partially immobilised.

'Leave it, Zade, come on this way,' Pip shouted. 'We can't push it over, it's too strong.' He tugged at Zade's arm. Pip led the way and took the girls back over the bridge. Zade turned and followed his companions, slightly confused as to why Pip didn't help him.

'Where are you going, you fool? Come back,' Zade called out breathlessly as he followed. 'Why are we going back this way?' Pip didn't answer. Zade craned his neck and looked over his shoulder to see if the robot was in pursuit. He felt a sinking feeling in the pit of his stomach; it was following them. How did it get up so quickly? he pondered. It looked even more sinister now with one arm, only a socket where the other arm should be. One thing to their advantage, though, was that it wasn't moving as fast. He turned away and caught up with the others.

This feels like the bloody movie, The Terminator, he thought, at that moment put him off science fiction films for life.

They reached the end of the corridor and Pip stood waiting. He looked as if he had a plan.

'Why are we stopping? That thing is still coming for us,' the two girls asked as they ran past him. Zade asked the same question when he finally arrived.

'Come on, Pip, let's get out of here. What are you waiting for now?' he said, glaring at him. 'We could have had that machine back there.'

'Look, listen to me. I just thought, it's the same as last time. That clockwork thing has to come over in single file. It's only got one arm. Last time he climbed underneath – but with one arm I doubt it would risk it,' Pip reasoned.

'So, why didn't we finish it off when I had it on the floor?' Zade argued. 'We could have finished it off there and then.'

'I don't know. Maybe I panicked, I was scared, all right,' he admitted. 'But, thinking about it now, we've got more chance of pushing it over the bridge with the four of us here. It can't fight all of us, can it?' Pip said, almost doubting his words as he said them.

'Oh my God,' Tina gasped and everyone turned to see what the matter was. 'It's not over there, it's gone!'

They looked on in surprise.

'Not again. I knew we should have finished it off when we had the chance,' Zade repeated. 'How agile is this thing?'

'It obviously doesn't have to come over the bridge then, does it?' Meadow said sceptically. 'So where is it? It obviously knows its way around here. Oh my God, it could jump out at any moment.'

'We've got to keep moving, it's too late to make a plan,' Zade uttered, eyes darting all around and shaking his head in disbelief. 'We should have finished it off over the other side,' he kept repeating.

'All right—all right, I made a mistake, I'm sorry,' Pip retorted, regretting his decision to leave it. 'We should go,' he said determinedly.

'But where?' Tina asked. 'We could run straight into it. It could actually be close by and we wouldn't even know it.'

'She's right,' Meadow chirped up. 'We've messed this up big time.'

'I've messed this up big time, Med, I know,' said Pip. 'Let's move on then, back to the clock, but keeping our wits about us at all times.'

'Whe're going back to the clock?' Zade asked, slightly confused.

'Yeah, we have to find a way out of this mad house somehow,' Pip reiterated, knowing he was back to square one in Zade's book of disapproval.

'Sounds like a plan to me,' Meadow agreed, siding with her boyfriend.

Zade gave her an awkward glance.

'Well what do you suggest?' Meadow asked.

Zade just shook his head. He was at a loss. 'Everyone, keep your eyes peeled for that mechanical monster, it could be anywhere,' he said. He didn't refer to the problem with Pip any more. They moved off trying to retrace their steps back to the clock and beyond. They were nervous, peering at every stairwell, corner and corridor. There was a deep feeling of dread in all of them.

'Where is he?' Tina whispered to Meadow. 'I hate this place, I much preferred it when I could see that beast.'

Meadow smiled a nervous smile to her friend.

They approached a narrow area. There was a passageway gutting its way through a sequence of stairs on either side. Pip was unsure which way to go when he came to it.

'I don't recognise this at all,' Zade said in a doubtful tone. It would be a great place for an ambush, he thought.

'I've never seen this part before either,' Pip answered truthfully. 'But—' He collapsed onto the floor before he could say anything else!

There was no time to take in what had happened. The one-armed clockwork robot swiftly stepped out of the shadows. By the time Zade recognised the situation the robot was onto him too. It gave a sweeping blow to his abdomen, which knocked the wind right out of his lungs. He crumpled to the floor like a discarded newspaper, gasping for breath, almost choking the sound of the girls' screams ringing in his ears. Pip was out cold there were spots of blood peppering the steel walkway beside his head.

Zade was trying to recover; he knew the girls were next and couldn't let that happen. The robot was relentless and knelt beside him. It gripped his throat and began the slow task of strangulation with its one remaining hand. Zade was helpless, Tina and Meadow saw what was happening and didn't know what to do. Shocked and scared and pumping with adrenaline they dived at the robot.

Tina managed to pull its head back and Meadow was clinging onto its only arm. She tried with all her might to release it from Zade's throat. But it was of no use, in two swift movements it released its clamp on Zade and tossed Meadow to one side. Then with a sweeping action it swivelled around, leaving its lower body facing forward. It knocked Tina backwards onto the platform, before returning and resuming what it was originally doing.

Zade, though, had partly recovered and grabbed it before it had a chance to grip his neck again. He grasped the robot's wrist with both hands and held fast. Even with the strength of both hands it was too strong this time to push it away. Its metal fingers splayed slowly and edged its way to his exposed throat. Zade was using all his muscle power just to slow down the surge of energy. The nerves in his arms were straining and stretching. He let out a slow groan. He held out for as long as he could but the machine was too strong. Its wriggling fingers pushed forward like a spider homing in on its prey. Zade kept grunting and gasping under the immense force, his eyes wide with terror of what would happen if he eased off. Finally, he couldn't hold back any longer and the robot gripped around his neck for the second and final time. The intricate system of its moving parts allowed it to gently clamped tighter and tighter.

Zade was slowly choking; the being had no emotion on his shiny, blank face and continued to close its fingers like a vice. The thumping of his heart felt as though it was exploding inside his head. The boom-boom-boom of his pulse filled his ears and his blood pressure was rendering him unconscious. He felt that his eyes were going to burst. He tried to speak. The grip he'd had on the robot's arm was meek and floppy now. The room began to spin like a roulette wheel. He couldn't hear anything around him and felt his eyelids slowly closing. A strangled squeal left his lips and the last gasp of air escaped his mouth.

A peace washed over his body and he was dreaming. He felt comfortable and warm, and away from any troubles. He was in a room that looked like a hospital ward. He saw strip lights and three beds around him, with Tina, Meadow, and Pip lying there. They were all sleeping with wires attached to their heads. He was confused and felt at peace. What was this?

Slowly, darkness clouded his vision, blacker and blacker the veil dropped and then nothing...

Chapter 16

Compartment

'Well, he's breathing,' Tina said with a tremble in her voice. 'Thank god for that.'

'I think he's going to be all right. I've seen him like this before, when we were kids,' Meadow said. 'His body kind of shuts down,' she said knowingly. 'He'll come around later after a sleep.'

'He's had things like this happen to him before then?' Tina questioned curiously.

'Yeah, all the time when we were kids,' she said with a shake of the head, as if remembering specific things. 'I'm more concerned about Pip, he's bleeding.'

'Well he's stopped bleeding now, Med.' Tina was kneeling over him and checking the wound. 'It's only a few little drops, I think he'll be all right as well.'

'They're both going to wake up with a headache that's for sure,' Meadow said, ruffling her fingers through her jet-black hair.

'I'm tired,' Tina said with a heavy sigh. 'Well more than that, exhausted really.'

'I'm not surprised,' Meadow said. She looked at her with wondrous eyes. 'How on earth did you stop that – that thing from killing Zade? I'm still amazed,' Meadow asked, still reeling from the shock. 'I mean, you took on that monster and shut it down. Yay, one for the girls.' She clenched her fist and punched the air in victory.

'I don't know – I really don't,' said Tina. 'There was a place in its back, like a small compartment or something, you know, like the top of a jewellery box. That's the only reason why I saw it. The design was beautiful even though that monster was deadly, and killing my boyfriend in the process. There was a button to the side and in a panic I pushed it and it opened. I didn't even know what to do once I'd opened it. There were a lot of moving parts inside so, well, I grabbed the nearest lever, pulled it back, and snapped it off. That's all I did. The whole thing stopped working then and you saw it flop backwards after that. I just hope its dead.' She stared at the motionless hunk of metal; it still sent a shiver through her body. She walked over to it tentatively. It looked harmless enough now, but was it truly dead? None of the parts that worked before she threw the lever were moving. It still gave her the jitters though, being this close. A wry grin escaped the taught expression she'd been wearing for what seemed like forever. She touched her cheeks and jaw; it was good to feel safe for the moment. They'd been running and hiding for so long she thought she'd never smile again. She took a long, lingering look and thought, *I stopped it. Not the boys or even Meadow, it was me.* As she bathed in her glory, Meadow spoke and broke her train of thought. 'Let's get some sleep and deal with that later,' she said sleepily.

'What if, you know, more of them come?' Tina asked, still shivering at the thought.

'Teen, to be honest, our boyfriends are out cold. We're exhausted too; what can we do to defend ourselves anyway, if they come?' She shrugged her shoulders. 'There's nothing we can really do to stop them, is there? We may as well relax girlfriend.' Tina chuckled being called this.

'I see what you mean; sleep it is then.'

The two girls slumped back wherever they were sitting and drifted off into a smooth slumber. But before Tina eventually slept; she would blink her eyes open a couple of times… just to check it was dead.

'Teen! Teen, wake up! Wake up.' Tina slowly opened her eyes and the image before her was blurred at first but as she slowly focused, saw the face of her boyfriend, Zade, smiling at her. She sat up and hugged him. She looked around and saw that all of them were awake. Pip looked a bit worse for wear and Zade had a pale complexion from strangulation but an excited spark in his eyes. But to all intents and purposes they were all well. By the look of Meadow, she'd only just been woken too.

'Pip, you OK?' Meadow asked.

'I'm fine, but I've got a monster headache,' he said, touching the part of his scalp where the gash pulled at his skin.

'What is it, Zade, what are you so excited about? We're alive, but we are still in this hellhole,' Tina said bitterly. 'You look as if you're bursting to tell us something.'

'I have,' he replied. 'I really have and it's really important.'

'What is it Zade? Come on, you always do this to me, just spit it out.'

'When I was being strangled – thanks by the way to whoever killed that thing – who did kill it anyway?'

Meadow pointed toward Tina.

Zade smiled again. 'How on earth did you manage that?' He looked totally dumbfounded. 'I thought I was going to die.' He paused for a second and looked at her adoringly.

'Don't worry about how I did it, you idiot, just get on with your story first,' she said impatiently.

'Oh OK,' he said, snapping out of his train of thought. 'In the last moments when I was blanking out I saw something.' He made a gesture for them to crowd around him. 'I'm going to have to whisper to each of you because he's everywhere,' Zade said. So first he whispered into Tina's ear and then to the others, each in turn. 'I think I saw us all in a room, wired up to some kind of machine. He must have knocked us out or hypnotised us and linked us up. It felt so real. Everything we've seen so far must be an illusion. We've been running around inside a dream. I swear it.'

'You can't be serious?' Meadow gushed. 'All this time? That's hard to get my head around, are you sure, Zade?'

'I think he's right,' Pip said in agreement. 'I've been working on a theory like that for a while. I didn't say anything because obviously I wasn't sure.'

'So what does this mean?' Tina asked in confusion. 'How are we gonna make this work for us?'

'But, the robot was going to kill you,' Meadow said, still thinking back. 'So, it wouldn't have mattered when you were dead…' She realised what she'd said and it dawned on her that she could have lost her brother. 'Oh God,' she said with a biting sadness.

'Shh, I'm all right.' Zade put his finger to his lips. He whispered again, 'Maybe it wouldn't have killed me, Med. Perhaps it was about to stop before I'd lost consciousness,' he said, trying to assure her, and rested his hand on her shoulder. 'But, Tina stopped it before it had a chance to do it itself. We must have messed up the process. So in my semi-conscious state it must have revealed to me what Lord Darke was up to,' he said in a hushed voice.

'Again, I don't see what you're getting at,' Meadow probed. 'If this is a dream, how do we get out?'

'One of us or all of us has to die,' Pip cut in. 'This will hopefully wake us up into the real world. Our real bodies are locked in a room somewhere in this house. We are just a dream and everything around us is not real.' This sent a shudder of fear through all of them.

'We're all going to have to die?' Meadow whispered in response.

'Yes, I'm afraid so, Med,' Pip said, shuffling up beside her. He put his arm around her shoulder for comfort. 'It's the only way.'

'OK,' Tina said after a long silence, 'where and how do we do this?' She obviously had her head fixed on the problem. 'I'm ready, Zade.'

Zade smiled and winked at her.

'Let's find our way back to the bridge,' he said. 'But before we do this, let's get rid of this robot. We don't want it coming after us, do we?'

They agreed and with one big heave, pushed the metal body over the side. It made a couple of squeaks and scrapes as it tumbled and then… nothing. All four of them stood for a moment in thought, wondering if, by some awful miracle, it would come flying back at them. But it didn't and so they left.

None of them said a word as they made their way with Pip leading. It felt like the beginning of the end. Would this work? Could they really pull it off? Was Zade right in what he saw? They would have to trust him with their very lives. It felt hard even to breathe.

'I'm scared,' Tina eventually said to Zade, 'I don't know if I can do this.'

'Me too, Teen, but it's the only way to get out of here once and for all,' Zade said, turning to her.

It was a quiet walk from then on and it took a while but they found the bridge. It lay stretched out over a black canvas of nothingness. It looked more sinister now than it did earlier – long, narrow, and foreboding. Each teenager felt an electric current of nerves shoot through their entire bodies. This was going to be the hardest thing they'd ever done.

'I feel sick,' Meadow said in a low feathered voice. 'I… I can't.'

'Me too, Med,' Tina admitted. 'I feel the same way but we have to do this if it means freedom.'

The two boys said nothing at this point.

'H—How are we—' Meadow couldn't get the words out.

'Look, we did this earlier – jumping off the stairs, remember, but the bottom was only metres away because that's the way Darke wanted it,' said Zade. 'This time we can see that it's a long way down, and if we can do it before he realises, then we've made it.'

Suddenly Darke's voice exploded over them.

'What is the meaning of this? What are you all doing?' His voice travelled overhead. No one answered.

'He knows something is up,' Zade said. He turned to his friends and repeated, 'He knows and we have to do this to get away, before he realises what we're up to. You all understand this now, don't you?' he said commandingly. They each nodded in turn.

'What are you doing?' Lord Darke repeated.

Pip led the way and one by one they filed along the bridge until they were standing in the middle.

'I have more robots coming so you'd better move along now,' he called out, his voice sounding troubled, not sure what his captives had in mind.

'Who do you think you are, The Wizard of freaking Oz?' Zade spat back. 'You're not God. You're pathetic.'

They linked hands, gripping far more tightly than needed. Pip held Meadow's and she in turn held Tina's, and finally Tina grasped Zade.

'Ready?' Zade asked.

'No,' Tina answered with nervous smile, before nodding. The rest of them did the same and dipped under the handrail.

'Stop—stop. You mustn't do this, I forbid it!' said Lord Darke, his wild rantings echoing boundlessly across the dark sky. Before he had a chance to stop them the four teenagers let themselves fall forward. Their eyes were shut tight. Tears streamed down each of their faces.

'Stop—stop, you can't do this!' Darke's concerned anger echoed. 'I command you to stop.'

But it was too late as the teenagers were swallowed up by the darkness, and were gone!

'No! No! Come back.' Darke said, ranting. He could feel his control fading away. 'I am in charge here. You must listen to me. This is my house and I set the rules. Come back—come back.'

But his demands fell on deaf ears.

Chapter 17

Reality

Their eyes burst open in unison when they felt the surface. Huge gasps of air escaped from each of them, just like the gush from a leaky balloon. They looked around and saw exactly what Zade had told them he'd seen. They were on four hospital gurneys, wired up to a machine and linked to each other. Then they each saw Lord Darke; he was frantically trying to adjust something on the machine, muttering and cursing in his haste. It was a video game. They'd been programmed into a video adventure.

'Quickly, take the wires off before he does any more damage,' Zade said in a rather gravelly, but urgent voice. Light-headed and groggy, they did as they were told. They had wires connected with suckers to their heads and arms. When they pulled them off, the machine that had been purring away in the corner suddenly chirped and then died. They didn't have time to grab Lord Darke he was quick and they were still weak from their ordeal. He realised it was too late to put them back to sleep and so ran straight out of the door, locking it behind him. They sat up, and with heads spinning, took in their surroundings.

'I feel really weird, probably because we've been constantly playing this game in our heads,' Zade confessed, putting his hands down for support before he could fall out of bed.

'Yeah, he really did a number on us, didn't he?' Pip said. 'You all right, Zade?'

'Yeah, fine,' came his immediate reply.

Meadow couldn't even speak for a while, she felt sick and weak. Tina noticed and went to her assistance. For some reason she had recovered the quickest, but saying that, she was still a little wobbly herself, just not quite as bad as the others.

'You all right, hun?' she asked, rubbing Meadow's back, trying to bring her out of her induced coma.

'Yeah, I think so, what did this guy give us?' she mumbled. 'My head feels like someone hit it with a hammer.' She placed her right palm on her forehead. Tina smiled warmly and looked around the room. The only light was coming from long strip lights in the ceiling. The room itself had no windows and only one door. It was set up exactly the same as a hospital ward.

Boy, this guy is off his head, Tina thought.

'Who would go to this length to trap teenagers?' she said, looking at the others.

'I suppose this kind of thing is on the news all the time; I just don't bother listening to it most of the time,' Meadow said, the colour slowly coming back to her cheeks.

'Everyone all right?' Pip asked. 'I know you don't want to hear this but we have to move. God only knows what he has lined up for us outside.'

'I'm with Pip on this one, guys,' said Zade. 'We can't stay here any longer.'

Soon they heard the sound of a wooden shutter being slid back.

'No, no, no,' ranted Lord Darke. There was a spy hole slot just below the top of the door and he was peering through, his menacing eyes like lasers. He no longer looked like the charming host that had greeted them when they first arrived. He was cursing and shouting with venom in his voice. 'This wasn't supposed to happen! You must return to your beds and put the wires back on, or all of my work will be ruined!' he ranted. His mouth was hidden behind the door, but his eyes burned and widened with every evil suggestion.

'Open this door,' Meadow shouted at Lord Darke. 'You'll go to prison for this, you mental head. You can't go round kidnapping people, it's against the law and it's sick. Once we've gone to the police your little game will be found out.'

'Yeah, let us out of here,' they all cried. Zade was on his feet and making his way to the door. He looked Lord Darke straight in the eyes. 'Let us out now,' he half whispered.

'You can't leave. You must not leave. I forbid it,' Darke insisted.

'Oh, we're leaving all right. Now let us out or I'll smash this bloody door down,' Zade bellowed, hate and strength building up inside.

The shutter was hastily pushed back into place and the sound of diminishing footsteps thudded in the distance.

'Hey, get back here!' Tina screamed. 'Don't run away, you coward!'

'Somehow I don't think he's running away. Whatever he's created here, he won't want anyone else to find it,' Pip said softly. 'We have to find a way out on our own and quickly.'

'What are you saying?' Zade asked curiously. 'He's not running away? What do you think he's doing then?'

'He must have got actual machines that are real and not make-believe. Machines that are probably clockwork, or mechanical,' Pip surmised. 'He's obsessed with clocks, mechanisms and engines, so I wouldn't be surprised if he's gone to his workshop. I don't think he's going to let us go that easily. He's got this far with computer hypnotism and mind wiring. So the images he conjured up for us in our heads are probably real and inside the house somewhere,' he concluded.

'How do you know all this stuff?' Meadow probed.

'I'm just assuming, you've got to expect the worst from this guy. He's an evil genius. It's like a theme from a movie, only we're in it and its very much happening around us.' Pip looked focused on what he was saying.

'He's right, Med,' Zade cut in. 'We've pretty much been inside the frame of a bad sci-fi movie. Only now we've woken up and we're still there. He's not going to let us get away and spoil his years of work.'

'Get me out of here, Zade,' Tina said.

'Right, come on, Pip, let's get this open,' Zade said. They moved quickly to the door. 'It's not as solid as I thought it would be,' Zade said, examining the density of the door and the hinges.

'He probably didn't expect us to wake up. Look over there.' Pip pointed to four plastic drip bags in the corner of the room. Each one had its own mobile frame fixed with castors, ready to roll to each bed and hook up to the patients. 'He's obviously an expert in gaming and dabbles in neurology or something of that nature. Either way we're lucky to be alive right now. If we hadn't woken up from that hypnotic state, then who knows what would've happened?'

'I don't even want to think about that,' Meadow said with a shudder.

'Christ, he never intended to let us go, did he?' Tina said, shaking as tears welled up in her eyes.

'Come on, you two, we need a hand to push this door open,' Zade said, trying to steer their thoughts away from the horror story they were in. 'OK, everyone, push.' They heaved together, pressing hard against the door, but nothing happened. There was a creek and a slight disturbance, but nothing more.

'OK,' Zade said. 'I'm going to take a run at it, and as soon as I hit the door, push as hard as you can.' Zade walked towards the back wall of the small room.

'Do you want me to run at it too, Zade?' Pip asked.

'I don't think there's enough room for the both of us to charge, but I'm carrying a little bit more weight than you, so…' He grinned and shrugged.

'OK, I'm skinny, I know.'

For the first time in ages they all gave a little laugh.

'Ready?'

'Ready,' they answered.

Zade didn't have enough room to build up much of a head of steam. But he did power forward before he slammed against the door. The others were ready and as soon as he contacted the surface they all pushed like mad, but the door was stubborn and still didn't open.

'What now?' Meadow puffed.

'Right, let me think,' Zade said. He sat on the bed, a little dazed from the collision he'd just endured. He looked at the framework holding the drip bags. He looked at Pip who seemed to be thinking the same thing.

'What if we tried to lever the door at the same time as I hit it.'

Zade looked at Pip and he nodded. The boys went to the corner of the room and unhooked the bags from one of the poles. The pole was metal and adjustable for different heights, so they unscrewed the base with the casters on and tossed it to one side. The end result resembled what looked like a crow bar, with the hook on one end and a short shaft on the other. They did the same to a second pole so now Pip and the two girls had something to lever the door with.

'What's the plan?' Tina asked, looking a bit bewildered. Meadow too looked on vaguely. Zade peered at Pip.

'To be fair, Pip, you don't smash down a hospital door every day. We know what we're doing, but we haven't told the girls, have we?'

'What we're going to do is – well, if it works,' Pip said with trepidation, 'is, us three put the hook of these bars into the small gap in the right hand side of the door. The side with the door catch on. Again, Zade is going to run into it and... hopefully this time if we pull back on the levers at the same time the door should...' he said this with a small croak in his voice, 'should burst open.'

They set themselves up and pushed the hooks around the gap by the handle. Zade walked back as far as he could to the end of the room.

'Ready,' he said.

'Yeah, ready,' the others replied. There was a second's pause... then Zade ran as quickly as he could, hoping that the door would give way once he got there. He hit it and shut his eyes. They pulled and the door relented and buckled under the pressure, collapsing to the ground. Zade went flying with it, and ended up heaped on top. A cloud of dust swirled around them in a foggy haze for a couple of seconds but it soon cleared. There were a few groans and shakes of heads, but all in all they were fine. Pip and Tina helped Zade to his feet and dusted him down.

'We don't know where he is; he could be on his way back with weapons,' Meadow said, looking at them in desperation. They all stopped suddenly and listened. There it was, unwelcome, but definitely there. Somewhere in the bowels of the house there were rumblings that vibrated the floorboards, walls and ceilings. The sound like a large engine that you would probably find digging on a building site or rolling out tarmac. The sound of fear.

'Oh my God, what is that?' Tina gasped.

'I don't know, but it doesn't sound good to me,' Meadow said.

'Pip was right, let's get out of here,' Zade said.

'Which way though?' Tina asked looking both ways.

'Not that way,' Pip said, pointing ominously. They started running away from the sound and away from danger, they hoped.

'Hold on a minute.' Zade had noticed a coil of rope, hung up on a fixing on the wall. He scooped it up and slipped it over his shoulder, like a climber would.

'What are you going to do with that?' Tina asked.

'I don't know yet, but we may need it later.'

'Come on, Zade, there's no time,' Pip insisted.

'OK, I'm ready, let's go,' he said once he'd secured it. They ran along the corridor, which somehow felt familiar. If they didn't know any better they would have thought they were still dreaming. But this was no dream. The passage opened out into a massive arena.

'Wow, this can't be the house! Are we still dreaming?' Pip asked with wonder.

'Nope, you're not dreaming,' she smiled as best she could.

'I don't see any windows, Pip. This must be underneath the house,' Zade said, darting his gaze in every direction. Just like in their dream there was a vast network of platforms, steps, and bridges.

'Oh my God,' Tina and Meadow said, gasping in awe. 'He's set this up exactly the same as our nightmare. How can someone do that?'

'We've gone from one crazy world into another. I can't take any more, Teen,' Meadow said, crying again. 'We're not getting home, are we?'

'The difference is, Med, this isn't a dream any more. Now we do this for real, so doors aren't going to disappear,' Pip reassured her. 'Floors aren't going to magically turn to liquid. That was all in our heads. We control this now. We set the rules for a change.'

The rumbling sound of an engine was louder now.

'That's so close,' Zade said scanning the area.

'There, look,' Tina pointed above.

Their worst fears were recognised. There, up on one of the platforms, was what could only be described as a mechanical robotic frame, with Lord Darke inside it, in full control. The whole thing was being gradually lowered to the ground in a huge cage and the madman was ready to kill. They all looked on with eyes wide and mouths fully open.

'Good grief,' Pip said, 'he's coming!'.

Chapter 18

No Escape

'This guy means business,' Tina gushed in horror.

'Look, he's slowly coming down to floor level so, when he's between floors and out of view, we go up,' Zade suggested. 'That way he won't have time to adjust and we can have a lead on him, for how long though, I don't know.'

'Sounds good to me,' Pip agreed. 'Any advantage we can take, well I'm up for that.' A nod each from the girls cemented it.

'Get ready, when he's halfway – we'll go,' Zade said. He was scrutinising the speed of descent and paused. 'Come on, come on,' he mumbled under his breath; it seemed to take an age. 'Go!'

They ran across the ground and up the first set of steps they came across. The stairwells were extra wide to what they had experienced earlier. The girls were in front and the boys followed.

'Go on, girls! Go up to the very top, don't stop,' Pip shouted from below.

'Why are these stairs so wide?' Meadow asked. No one had the answer.

There was an echoed clang below, which vibrated its way through the body of the structure. Zade stopped for a moment and flicked a gaze over his shoulder; he wished he hadn't. His heart sank. 'Can we ever get a break,' he hissed.

Darke's evil machine stepped out of the cage, like a king stepping off its throne. The robot body was big, at least ten feet high. Darke was housed in the middle to upper half. The whole thing was like the clockwork robots they'd seen in their dream state; it had a torso, arms, legs, and the head was the lookout point for the evil lord. From what Zade could make out there wasn't only one source of power, meaning it looked like a clockwork-cum-hydraulic mishmash. It was powerful and ready for battle too. Through each of the limbs Zade could see pipes snaking through the inner parts, amongst a fully working cog system. The outer skin was a mesh compound, which allowed anyone to see the inner workings. Zade didn't have time to look any longer and followed the others. Darke saw him and peered into his eyes, before he flitted away. Darke could also see movement in the upper structure. He quickly addressed them through a microphone built into the chest of the beast. His booming voice filled the whole underground cavern.

'You won't escape me down here!' There was a tone of excitement to his voice. 'There is no escape,' he bellowed, and as he did so the tunnel, where they'd entered the arena, slammed shut!

'Oh God,' Tina squeaked as the vibration shook through the framework again.

'He's controlling everything from inside that damn machine,' Pip shouted breathlessly.

The next thing they felt was another huge shudder. Darke's robot was making its way up the stairwell, one step at a time.

'Run, rabbits, run,' he chuckled as he ascended.

'That's why these stairways are so wide, he can go anywhere with that thing,' Meadow figured out with a sinking heart. 'There is no escape.'

'Keep on climbing Med,' Zade and Pip said. They were just behind them encouraging them all the way. 'He's got to catch us first, and we're not going to make that easy for him,' he gasped breathlessly.

Clang-clang-clang! The metal monster continued its pursuit, vapours pouring out of vents fixed to the upper-back section. There was a burst of steam with every movement.

'Look, I know I've been against this all along but we would have more chance if we split up into pairs,' Zade admitted as they neared the top. 'Two sets of people are going to be harder to catch with his restricted movements.'

'B—but you said stick together from now on,' Tina sobbed, feeling exhausted.

Zade mulled it over and shook his head.

'OK, let's find somewhere to hide and we can figure out a way of stopping this thing,' Zade suggested. 'Stop for a moment, he'll take a while to get up here. I've got another plan.'

'What is it?' Tina asked meekly.

'Hold it a minute and let me think.' He closed his eyes and bobbed his head from side to side, as if running some ideas through his mind. 'OK, OK, this rope is strong and there's plenty of it. What if we laid it in a big loop on one of these stairs, so it can't be seen? One of us can act as decoy – I'll do it.' Zade put his hand on his chest. 'When he sees me, and without looking down, maybe he'll step into the loop you lot can pull the other end. This will hopefully put him off balance. What do you think?'

There was an awkward silence.

'It does actually sound as if it'll work,' Meadow piped up.

'OK then, let's go,' said Zade. He unhitched the rope from his shoulder and set it into a noose. He spread the whole loop along the second step from the top and trailed the rest of the rope to one side. It was a work of genius; the trap was almost invisible unless you were actually looking for it. He stood pleased with himself.

Then the damning sound of Darke's machine loomed in the background.

'Right, are you three ready? You know what to do?' he whispered and they gave him a very nervous thumbs up.

He waited for Darke to get to the bottom of the steps. Then, he climed halfway up. Zade ran across the top in the line of sight. Lord Darke's eyes flashed with excitement.

'Got you now, boy,' he said. He climbed up one, two, three steps and, as he stepped onto the last one before the top, he got snagged! The left leg of his machine was already on the top step but for some reason he couldn't lift his right leg.

'What the devil is going on?' he said to himself in confusion. He looked strangely down at his instruments. The pressure needle for his right limb was surprisingly high. The more he pushed the lever to lift, the more his machine groaned at the strain. He felt it shift and begin to topple off balance.

'What's happening?' he shouted in astonishment as his beloved robot fell backwards. It fell towards the floor and tumbled to the bottom of the stairs. It finally came to a halt with a crunch.

Zade had already joined the others to pull on the rope and once the mechanical man had fallen they all appeared on the top of the steps. Lord Darke's robot was on its back, helpless, it seemed.

'Let's go now and get him,' Pip said, 'before he has a chance to get back up.' They ran down to it but the robot began to right itself. They stopped in sheer frustration. It only took moments and Darke was back on his metal legs, strong as ever.

'Damn!' Meadow cursed. 'It's too late.'

'Come on, we've no time, let's go,' Zade screeched. 'It didn't work. Damn, damn, damn!'

They had no choice now but to run, so once more they turned and ran away. They could outrun Darke, but for how long? Again they had a good distance between him and they stopped for a breath.

Then Pip spoke up. 'Zade, Med, Tina, listen to me. That thing is made up of pipes with fluid inside. It has clockwork parts too, by the look of it. If you can distract him so that he follows you three, thinking it's the four of us. I can sneak up behind and rip one of those pipes off. He'll be disabled, properly. Zade's plan was a good one.' He looked at his friend and smiled. 'But we didn't expect Darke to recover so quickly. This way it will disable him completely, if it works. It's a plan. It'll take him a while to fix it and we'll have more chance to get away, or take care of him.' Pip looked at the fear on their faces and it only matched his own. 'There is no other way. If his machine is broken, he'll have to get out and that will be our chance to either stop him or find a way out.'

'He's right, girls. Pip knows what he's talking about. He does this kind of thing in classes at school. I didn't take much notice in my engineering class, so I'm at a loss,' Zade said, kicking himself for not listening to Mr Evans in lessons.

The churning and grinding sound of Darkes machine was getting closer.

'Are we all agreed on my plan?' Pip reiterated.

'Agreed.' Tina, Meadow and Zade looked at one another and back at Pip.

'OK, we'll make our way over to the other side there.' Pip pointed to an area where he could split off from the others without being noticed. 'You lot keep going and I'll follow behind. I only hope that this Lord Darke character doesn't have a rearview mirror or camera to his robot and sees me following. If he does then it's game over. OK, he's coming. Let's go.'

They took off in the direction that Pip stipulated. He hung back until he got the chance to slip away. He then dived into a darkened corner and huddled up into a ball. He had to hold on to the metal beside him, to stop from sliding out in front of the advancing clockwork man. The huge impact of every footstep made it almost impossible to keep hidden. It shook the foundations to the point in which Pip thought the whole structure would collapse. Darke's machine banged onwards.

It was right next to him when it stopped. Pip froze; he could hardly breathe. The smell of engine oil and pungent steam filled the air. He felt like coughing but held back and cupped his hand over his mouth. The machine hissed a sigh of relief and the rowdy workings settled for a moment.

Why has he stopped here? Pip thought. *He knows I'm here. He knows I'm hiding.* Pip was already freaking out and was ready to slide out into the open and give himself up. But he waited as Darke did nothing for a moment; he just stood there. *He would have got me by now,* he thought. *What's he doing?*

Pip peered through the twisted lattice steelwork and could see Lord Darke's face directly head-on through a spy hole. The face of Darke's creation had a visor that gave him a panoramic view of his surroundings. Darke looked bewildered and in a heart-stopping moment looked straight into Pip's eyes.

Pip sucked in air, closed his mouth, and held his breath. He tried even not to blink. He felt like he could scream.

Lord Darke leaned forward and Pip almost cried out. It was as if he was looking right through him not focusing on anything in particular. But just as quickly, he turned away. The robot sprang back into action and the *bang, bang, bang* of Darke's machine continued in the direction that the others had taken.

Pip was almost sick. His breathing was rapid and his heart was beating faster than a speeding train.

'God, that was close,' he gulped.

'You can't hide from me; it's only a matter of time before I get the lot of you. I'll sort you out for messing up my game,' he said. 'I see you now,' he growled as he let out a great big belly laugh. 'There's definitely no escape once you cross that bridge.'

Then the three in front realised he was right. They'd just run over the bridge, but this one came to a dead end. There was only one platform above it with a set of steps on both sides leading to the top, but that was it. No way out.

'Oh my God,' Tina squeaked breathlessly as she, Meadow, and Zade came to a full stop. 'There's nowhere to go from here.' She peered over the side and was nearly sick. There was a long, long drop to the ground from their height and a shudder went right through her. Lord Darke was advancing, driving his deadly mechanical robot towards them. The heavy impact on the bridge was menacing enough, without its huge frame almost blotting out the background. *Clang-clang-clang-clang.* It powered on.

'Nowhere to go, nowhere to run,' he said with a chuckle. 'Thought you could get away from me, did you? Once in my world there is no escape, little ones.' His condescending tone was sickening.

'Come on, Pip, do your stuff,' Zade whispered in encouragement. 'Don't let us down now.' Zade was having second thoughts. This could be a trick. Pip could have had a second plan all along and now was making his way to the exit. *I'm sure he wouldn't let us down now, after all we've been through together*, he thought. He stopped and shut everything else out. *Where are you Pip? You should be here by now.*

Shhh-bang shhh-bang shhh-bang. Darke was here. Zade never felt so helpless. He had his sister and girlfriend to protect, but he couldn't against this monster. He would have to rush it on his own.

'Let's hope that Pip is all right and he has the power to stop this bloody thing, girls,' Zade said with fear written all over his face. 'OK, girls, get behind me.'

Lord Dark knew that they were trapped and was closing at a steady pace. A smile filled his evil face, the power and the control – they were doomed!

Chapter 19

Combat

'Where's Pip?' Meadow asked anxiously, biting at her lip. 'Where are you?' she mumbled to herself.

'I don't know, but he'd better move quickly,' said Zade. 'We've run out of time.' He stared at Meadow and Tina with scepticism. The vibration of the heavy-footed robot was shaking the whole structure of the bridge. So, they had to hold on tight to the handrail just to stay upright.

'Pip, come on, come on,' Zade whispered. 'Don't let us down, don't let us down.' Lord Darke had a couple of steps and he would be on the bridge.

'Your mine now,' he chuckled through his megaphone.

'Look, when he eventually gets on this bridge, we can, if we're quick, run past him,' Zade said in hope more than anything.

'Really?' the two girls replied, not sounding too confident.

'He's not going to let that happen, is he?' Tina added. With that, Lord Darke stopped at the edge of the bridge, with a whoosh of steam and a clank. They could see he was preoccupied in the cockpit. He pressed a couple of buttons on his control panel and the three trapped teenagers looked on in curiosity. He looked perturbed and his brow creased in annoyance, but then relaxed and smiled.

'What's he doing? Maybe he's stuck,' Tina said with a burst of excitement, but before anyone could answer a compartment opened up in the left leg of the machine and a ball rolled out. It was the size of a beach ball and bounced off the side and onto the platform until it stopped. Zade and the others looked on in amusement until they saw what it was about to do. Two legs popped out, one on either side and lifted the ball off the floor. At the top of the sphere a single arm erected like an antenna and sprouted four blades that began rotating at speed. The legs began to move and started walking beside its 'mother'.

'The git, he's sealed every escape route. Now we really are trapped,' Zade gulped.

'Escape now, my beauties,' said Darke, his scratchy voice exploding over the megaphone and letting out a huge, sickly belly laugh. Darke's machine clunked back into action and with the little bot at its side, started across the bridge.

'What are we *going to do*, Zade?' Meadow barked hysterically.

'We can't stop this!' Tina screamed. Zade looked on helplessly panic building up in his throat. He couldn't attack the small droid because he didn't have a weapon to break the blades, it would cut him to pieces. Lord Darke's machine was far too powerful to even try and take on. Even if he had Pip by his side it wouldn't really matter. It didn't look good. He could feel the end nearing. *Hold it together, Zade, get a grip*, he told himself. So he again pushed his sister and girlfriend behind him and stood his ground. He didn't feel brave in any shape or form. He had two of the people he loved most in the world behind him and… he couldn't protect them. He felt sick.

Darke was moving closer by the second, his minibot at his side. Things then began to change. In a strange limping movement, Lord Darke's robot was struggling to move its left leg. It could only sort of bounce its right leg in front and drag the left behind. Darke himself was manically trying to get his clockwork machine to continue to walk forward but it just wouldn't. Then the teenagers could see the reason why, the mystery was revealing itself.

'Look Zade, behind its left leg,' Meadow said. She was jumping on the spot, as if she needed to go to the loo.

'Wha—what,' Zade was about to ask, then he saw for himself. There was green liquid oozing out of a pipe in its lower limb. Pip was also clearly visible to everyone as he again was trying to pull at a pipe in the right limb. Darke was onto him though, and swung the robot's right arm, swatting him like a fly. Pip, taken totally by surprise, went tumbling backwards and crash landed on the steel platform. Now though, he'd swivelled completely to a one hundred and eighty degree turn and was facing away from the stranded teenagers.

'Get away from my machine, you fool,' Darke bellowed, eyes raging and teeth bared. At this point Zade took his chance. Darke was in confusion and had lifted the robot's right leg until it was in mid-air and balancing precariously; in fact the whole machine was leaning back. Zade raced forward, and with all his weight, sprang off the ground and dived onto the android. This took Lord Darke by surprise and with the shift in weight the whole thing toppled over backwards and fell towards Pip. He was still dazed from the blow he'd only just received, but coming around he rolled out of the way just in time to avoid being flattened. Darke pushed his robot off the steel floor in a press up kind of lift. Soon Darke's robot had righted itself and rotated back into its original position, knocking Zade off in the frenzy. Zade grappled with Darke but the maniac was too quick for the youngster. Zade soon found himself being lifted into the air, the robot's right arm had gripped the material on his t-shirt and wouldn't let go. Darke laughed as he dangled the youngster in front of him.

'Help!' he screamed as his body was hoisted and the outstretched arm lifted him over the side. Lord Darke beamed a wide grin. He then pressed the button to release the handgrip to the screams of the girls. Zade didn't want to die but felt the end was moments away. He struggled to reach for the handrail, but it was too far away. He closed his eyes and waited for the inevitable drop… but it didn't happen. He was suddenly drenched in a warm, green oily liquid as it spewed from another broken hydraulic vein in the robot's arm.

'He can't drop you, Zade, the robots hand is clasped shut now,' Pip shouted in triumph. Tina and Meadow ran past the robot and Meadow kicked out at the small bot that stood in her way. She knocked it completely over the side and out of sight.

'What have you done?!' Darke bellowed. He was livid, every vein in his face raised to explode. He frantically punched at his keyboard and raised the robot's left arm to pummel Pip to a pulp. But to his dismay, Pip grabbed the arm and clung on for dear life. It was a ridiculous situation, Zade dangling precariously over the side and Pip swinging around like a piece of sticky chewing gum someone was trying to throw away.

'Help me, girls! Help me!' Pip shouted as he was swinging from side to side.

'Med, Tina, grab the pipe,' Zade said. He looked on helplessly as he hung on too. There were moans and groans emanating from inside the robot's guts. The machine itself was wearing out its own gears and cogs.

'Don't let go, Pip,' Zade called out. 'We've got him if you can only hold on.'

'Huh, are you nuts. What else am I supposed to do?' he screamed back.

'Teen, get onto its arm with me,' Meadow shouted with excitement and the two girls dived onto the end of the limb next to Pip. Darke looked on in dread. He was losing this battle and he knew it. No matter what he tried to compensate inside his cockpit, it made no difference.

'Brilliant,' Zade called with words of encouragement. The combined weight of both girls, which admittedly wasn't much, plus the weight of Pip hanging on the end was enough to slow the arm down and stop it from thrashing about. Eventually, the leaking oil from the rest of the system rendered the left arm useless as well. The robot was now pooled in its own fluid.

'Oh my God, that was totally mental,' Tina said and started laughing. 'We're winning, we're winning,' she repeated.

'You're mental,' Meadow added and saw the funny side and started laughing too. 'He doesn't look too happy in there,' she said with a grin.

Finally, apart from a right leg that was stamping manically, the robot was disarmed. The leg stopped its stomping when the last of the fluid drained away. Lord Darke was in so much of a frenzy that he tried to get up and out of his prized machine. He thrust his head on the visor in his haste and knocked himself out cold.

'Well that can't be a bad thing,' Tina said in relief. 'For once in this crazy house we're in control now.' Pip managed to climb over the whole mangled wreck and switched the thing off. The clockwork system drew to a halt and to all intents and purposes… it was dead. Huge sighs were heard all around.

'Thank God for that,' gasped Tina.

'Yeah, wow,' replied Meadow.

It went quiet for a moment of sheer piece.

'Yeah, hello, I'm still here you know,' Zade called out and they all shot back into focus.

'Oh, good grief,' Pip said as he realised the danger Zade was still in. 'Come on, girls, give me a hand to get him back in.' He reached out and Zade grabbed his hand just as the material gave way. The girls gripped his other arm and heaved him back onto the bridge. He sat down and gasped.

'You're safe now, Zade,' Tina whispered tenderly.

'I don't believe we got away with that,' Zade said softly. 'I thought we were gonners for sure.'

'What a bloody nightmare,' Meadow said with a puff, 'and we still haven't got out of this place yet.'

Pip couldn't speak; he was too exhausted by the ordeal and collapsed next to Zade. He shook his head and Zade patted him on the back.

'Well done, boy,' he said in appreciation.

'Hey, look at that. That's strange,' Meadow said as she squinted at Lord Darke's unconscious face.

'Look at what?' Tina asked, half in a world of her own. 'Who wants to look at that crazy fool?' Tina wasn't interested in Darke any more. She only wanted to escape to safety and see the outside world again.

'Eek, his skin has sort of peeled off and it's silver underneath,' she said curiously. 'Look it's all hanging and squidgy.

'Uh,' Pip was onto it straight away. His inventive mind was working overtime. He quickly felt around the rim of the helmet and found a release button. When he pressed it, a gush of air escaped and the top of the robot's head popped open. He reached in and nervously touched the flap of skin that hung loosely on Lord Darke's face. He examined it for a moment.

'Good grief,' he spluttered his eyes wide. It wasn't skin at all, but some kind of rubber component. When he pulled on it, squeamishly at first, it tore away.

'Yuck!' Tina wretched.

'Double yuk,' Meadow agreed. 'What is that?' Her face reflected her squeamish side.

'He's a robot too.' Pip was fascinated and stared at the technology. 'Unbelievable.'

'Come on,' Zade urged, 'there's no time to examime it, we've got to go.'

Chapter 20

Hope

'Well, with Lord Darke being a robot, who is controlling him?' Meadow asked. 'There must be someone else.'

'This is a whole different ball game now,' Pip responded. 'And we thought we'd won.'

'Yeah, we're dealing with a whole other enemy now,' Zade said. He looked at Pip, who understood the danger they were still in.

'You've destroyed everything, my life's work.' A voice boomed over the speaker system.

They all looked at one another in bewilderment.

'Who are you?' Zade shouted. 'And what do you want from us. We've played your little game. Now let us go.'

'I am old and tired,' the voice continued in response.

'You're sick is what you are' Tina added. 'Let us go.'

'I'm afraid I can't do that,' came the ominous reply rebounding around their ears.

'What do you mean... can't?' Pip joined in. 'You can do what you want to do. You don't need us any more. We've satisfied you with entertainment, now let us go.'

'I can't let anyone know about this place, I would have police searching all over my house and I'm not standing for that,' he said sternly. 'You can't leave and that's final.'

'You can't keep people locked away,' Meadow retaliated. 'The police will come looking eventually. We're four teenagers, and that's not going to go unnoticed.'

'Exactly. That's why I can't let you go,' the voice said. 'Face it, you're trapped here, forever!'

'We'll find a way out eventually and then you won't stop us leaving,' Zade responded defiantly.

'I was hoping you wouldn't say that. I was hoping that you would play my little games until you were too old to leave.'

'Can't you just listen to yourself? You can't keep people prisoner for your entertainment, to bring them out, like a toy out of a box,' Tina said, getting annoyed. 'What are you some kind of man that never grew up or something?'

'This is my house and you belong to me now!' he answered. 'I'm not giving you away to anyone else. If I can't have you then no one will.'

'My God, he's off his head,' Meadow said, looking at the others. 'Let's go now.'

'Let us out!' Pip shouted. 'I've had it.'

'No you can't.' He changed his approach. 'I'll have food brought to you and we can talk some more. You must be tired. Why not sleep and we'll discuss this later?' His voice softened. 'Don't be upset, this can be a really nice place to be.'

'Y—yeah, OK.' Pip replied, before whispering. 'I've seen this type of thing before in movies. The evil host can't let go and the victims are locked away, forever. We've got to make him think we're going along with his plan.' Then he whispered into Zade's ear, 'When he thinks he's got us, we'll make our move and escape.'

Zade nodded.

'Splendid,' the voice answered and then said no more.

'What are you doing?' Tina said, staring at Pip with contempt. He put his finger to his lips and shook his head.

'Let's humour him for now. Let him get on with making food and we can try and find a way out,' he said.

'How? He has all the exits closed and everything is under his control,' Zade said with distaste. 'We're stuck in this underground tomb.'

'Exactly,' Pip said with a real sparkle in his eye.

'What?' Meadow cut in. 'I'm lost now, what are you on about.'

'Yeah, spit it out.' Tina was in no mood for riddles. 'If you've got a plan, Pip... tell me.'

'Likewise,' Zade added.

'Well, we're underground and there has to be ventilation. I mean, we're breathing air, aren't we? So there has got to be a venting system or some kind of big pipework that leads to the surface,' he said.

Zade nodded in agreement, wishing he'd thought of such an obvious solution.

'Makes sense, but you've already sussed this out, haven't you?' Zade asked.

'Look over there.' He pointed to a big vent fixed into the wall high up in the ceiling. They could barely see it with all the tangle of metal framework. 'All we have to do is get over there and climb in,' he said simply. 'Once we're in there, we just follow the line until we're outside.'

'Let's do it before he realises,' Zade said; he was as anxious as everyone else to get out.

'We don't know how long he's going to take with food preparation, so we can't waste any more time,' Pip urged.

They moved quickly along the labyrinth of steel pathways and stairwells that ascended the heights. When they came to the place where vent was situated they stopped. As luck would have it, it was only a matter of climbing onto a maintenance ladder and climbing in after they'd pulled off the cover. Pip and Zade stepped up the ladder on each side of the vent. The cover itself was about the size in of a large wheelie bin lid.

'Well, we can all fit in there, size-wise,' Zade observed.

'Yeah, but will it hold our combined weight once we're all moving along in there?' Pip asked, looking doubtful.

'What are you doing up there?' Meadow called out in a high-pitched hiss.

'Med, shut up, you mad head. Do you want the old mental man to catch us?' Zade scolded in a whisper.

'There's only one shot we get at this, Pip. We'll have to climb inside and spread ourselves out to distribute the weight,' Zade said, sounding chuffed with himself.

'Wow, I'm impressed,' Pip came back.

'All right, smart pants, shut up. I can still knock you're block off, you know.' Pip went a little red in the face and said no more. Both boys grabbed the cover while the girls supported them from the floor. It took a bit of a struggle to remove it but it eventually gave in and they handed it down to the girls, who gently put it onto the platform as quietly as they could.

'That was awkward,' Tina commented.

'Yeah, well this manual stuff should normally be man's work,' Meadow said, grinning. 'Girls should be in charge and give out the orders.'

'Do you want to go in first, Zade?' Pip asked, you're braver than me.'

'OK, no problem.' Zade shrugged his shoulders. Inside, it was dark and smelly and none of them really wanted to enter. Zade climbed inside followed by Meadow.

'Where the hell does this lead?' Meadow cursed, clambering in behind her brother.

'I have no idea, Med, but it has got to be better than where we've been for the last...' he paused. He couldn't remember how long they'd been there.

'Wha—what is it, Zade?' asked Meadow, worried that something may have happened to him in there.

'Well, I mean, how long have we actually been in this place? I can't remember,' he eventually said through the darkness.

'I don't know and I don't care. Let's not worry about that now.'

'Are we all in yet?' Zade's voice echoed from further inside.

'Yes, I'm in,' Tina answered.

'Yeah, I'm just behind her,' Pip called.

'You'd better not be looking at her butt, dude,' said Zade, his echo ringing through the vent.

'Zade, I can't even see my hand in front of my face, don't worry about anything else,' Pip replied.

Tina smiled in the darkness, feeling protected.

'OK then, let's find out where this place actually ends up,' said Zade. 'And try to keep it quiet.' He sounded excited as he shuffled forward like a mole. It was warm inside and the air was stale. The metal sections were warm to the touch. *Heat rises*, Zade thought.

'Oh, what is that smell?' Tina retched.

'That's Zade, Teen,' Meadow said in the darkness.

'Sorry,' Zade called from back. 'That was me.'

'You dirty Cow,' Meadow blasted, giving him a slap on the behind. Zade boyishly gave himself a little smile at what he'd just done. He nearly even giggled but thought better of it.

'Wow, what's that?' Pip heaved, getting the backlash. 'Can someone just remember that I'm the last in line here.'

'It's Zade,' Tina told him. 'Med, how come you haven't thrown up? That's horrible.'

'I'm used to my stinky brother, Teen. I've had to grow up with that smell. I must be immune. You'll get used to it eventually.' Tina wrinkled her nose and was happy the stale air was almost gone. *What am I getting myself into?* she thought as she shuffled along.

They made their way on hands and knees in the pitch black. Each began to sweat in the muggy atmosphere of the venting system.

'My throat is dry,' Meadow gagged.

'Mine too,' Tina complained.

'We're all thirsty, girls, but when we're outside we can get a drink. Now stop complaining and shut up,' Zade rasped.

Their shuffling knees and elbows would give away their position if their enemy was in earshot. Tina screamed and everyone stopped.

'What's happening?' Zade called from the front. 'Teen, you all right?' he said anxiously.

'Something landed on me,' she said, frantically trying to brush it off her face and hair.

'Tina, calm down, it's all right,' Meadow comforted in the heated darkness.

'Are you OK now,' Pip asked.

'Yeah, fine,' she said, realising it must have been a cobweb or something. 'I just want to get out of here.'

'We won't be long, Teen. It can't be far now, honest,' said Zade, trying to calm her.

'We good to go?' Meadow asked.

'Yeah,' Tina responded and added a nod which no one could see. They pushed along horizontally for a while until the pipe began to incline gently. The slope gradually got intense and so they had to push against the sides to keep moving.

I hope this doesn't get too steep, Zade pondered, *or we won't be able to climb.* He noticed that the pipe dropped off to a horizontal base, so he slipped inside. He could actually turn in this section and whispered to Meadow that he was reaching out for her. She extended her arm until she felt his hand and gripped on. He pulled her up and over the bend in the pipe. He turned and moved further along. Meadow did the same for Tina and she did the same for Pip. They continued their journey with grunting and moaning from all four of them.

Zade stopped, causing a chain reaction. Meadow headed into his butt and so on.

'Zade, what are you doing, you idiot?' she said in a high-pitched squeal.

'Hey, guys,' Zade whispered back, 'I think I can see light up there.'

'That's got to be a way out, right?' said Tina, her laboured voice coming from the middle of the train. Soon warmth filled her body.

'I hope so,' Pip added. The pipe again levelled off and it was easier for them to crawl. They moved on with more purpose and the light became stronger.

'Thank God for that,' Meadow said in relief. 'I never thought I would see light again.'

'Yeah, I know what you mean, Med. I never thought we'd ever get to the end,' Tina croaked from behind.

'Keep it down, will you? Whereever he is, he'll hear us and all this will be for nothing.' Zade shifted right up to the vent plate and peered through. He had to squint while his eyes got used to the light. His heart sank.

'Oh great,' he said ominously, gritting his teeth in frustration.

'What can you see? Zade, what is it?' they cried, making it harder to answer all of them.

'It's way too far down to climb out here, guys,' he said despondently. 'We're about ten to fifteen feet up. We'd kill ourselves trying to escape from here.'

'Hey, everyone?' Pip said, calling them back. 'Didn't anyone notice this hatch?' he said excitedly.

'What hatch?' Zade called back, 'I didn't see any hatch.'

Pip was too engaged in finding out to answer. He felt in the half-light and could feel a section of plate cut out of the wall. It had two clips that held the plate on. He simply unscrewed the wing nuts, one at a time, until they unscrewed and the section of the pipe fell away. Luckily for them it was on a hinge and only fell back like a trap door. Enough light flowed into the pipe to light up the segment they were in.

'What's there, Pip?' Zade whispered. 'Can we get out that way?' he asked anxiously.

'It's one of the halls with a balcony. We can climb out and hopefully make our way down; it's not too far to jump,' he squeaked with excitement. 'This is it, guys. A way out at last.'

'Good work, boyfriend,' Meadow said, filled with new hope.

'Let's go then,' Tina said, not wanting to stay in this dark, stale place any longer.

Pip slowly climbed out and, with the girls helping him down, he wriggled his legs until he could feel solid ground.

'It's not too far,' his voice echoed, even though he was whispering. 'Come on, Teen, you next.' She slowly eased out of the hole and let him guide her down.

'OK, let go. I've got you,' he said as she built up her courage and unclamped her hands. The next was Meadow, who came down fairly quickly, and finally Zade. They were all out, ready to escape. It was bright and airy and welcoming.

'Right, where do we go now?' Tina asked.

'Well the door is right there,' Pip said, pointing down the stairs. Meadow looked across the foyer to the entrance. Tears started rolling down her face.

'I can't believe it,' she said, eyes streaming. Tina hugged her and began crying too.

'Girls, we haven't got time for this, there's our chance,' Zade said. 'I don't like it, it's too easy. We keep our eyes and ears open. This guy is no fool. He won't leave us go that easily.'

'My brother, always the pessimist.' Meadow chirped.

'No, just careful,' he added.

'Yeah, let's get out of this nightmare once and for all,' said Pip. 'We can talk about who's after us after we get out.' *That made sense*, Tina thought.

'Come on, the door is waiting for us. We've finally made it,' Meadow chirped.

It was only a matter of quickly moving down the staircase to the bottom, then across the floor and out of the door to freedom.

'Come on—come on,' Zade said, herding them like a sheepdog guiding sheep, to the top step. It was hard to control their excitement.

'Where do you think you are going?'

Everyone froze.

Chapter 21

A Slim Chance

'You fools actually thought you could escape without me catching you?' The voice bellowed throughout the whole house, making the building feel alive.

'OK, he knows. Let's get the hell out,' Zade screeched.

'Stop where you are. One push of this button and the whole house will disintegrate.'

Zade stopped, unsure as to what to do.

'He's bluffing,' Pip said. 'Come on.' He nudged Zade's side.

'I don't think he is, Pip,' said Zade. 'He hasn't so far has he?'

'What do we do?' the girls asked, sobbing.

'I say call his bluff,' Pip was gambling on fate. 'He wouldn't blow up his own house. You lot with me?' He looked at them one by one. When they nodded in agreement Pip said, 'Let's go,' and grabbed Meadow's hand. Zade grabbed Tina's hand and they began to run down the stairs.

'You wouldn't listen, you fools,' came the voice was filled with anger. 'Goodbye,' he said simply.

Firstly there were small explosions that seemed to come from far within the bowels of Darke House. Everything shook with each blast, sending masonry, wood and glass showering down from the ceiling. The stairs underneath their feet cracked and broke away.

'He wasn't bluffing, Zade,' Tina screamed. 'He's actually going to blow the house up.'

'Hold on, we have to get out while we can,' said Zade. He was pulling her along like a toy puppy, but a huge gap appeared, too far to try and cross. Tina screamed.

'Zade, we're not going to make it,' Pip barked.

Pillars cracked, ceilings gave way as large chunks of masonry fell all around.'

'We have to go back?' said Pip. Even as he said the words, it hurt.

'Back? What do you mean back?' Zade shouted as Pip and Meadow retreated.

'The stairs on the other side are still intact. We can get out that way.'

Zade looked at Tina, her face was smudged in dust and streaked with tears. She looked terrified.

'Come on, let's follow them. Maybe we can get out that side,' said Zade. Tina nodded.

They chased behind his sister and her boyfriend. They ran across the balcony to the other set of stairs, all the time explosions erupting all over. Visibility was muted as clouds of dust appeared around them. Pip and Meadow were halfway down with Zade and Tina not far behind. Another blast rumbled the ground and a wide gap appeared between the two couples. Zade fell and Tina landed at his side.

'Pip!' Zade roared. 'Stop!'

Pip and Meadow looked back and saw their dilemma. They were almost at the bottom and just across the way was the entrance.

'Pip, we have to help them,' she shrieked. Dust and confusion reigned all around. The huge crack in the stairs was getting bigger.

'You're going to have to jump,' Pip called out.

'I—I can't, it's too far,' Tina cried.

'You've got to, Tina,' Meadow reacted. 'There's no other way and no time. Now come on, girl.'

'Go on,' Zade urged, 'take a run.'

Filled with fear and not knowing the outcome, she took a few steps back and ran. She took a huge leap, as if she was in a triple jump competition. Pip and Meadow grabbed her as she landed.

'Now you, Zade,' Pip said and reached out his hands. Zade did the same and took a few steps back. He broke into a downward sprint and as he pushed off from the jagged edge there was another explosion. He slipped and the gap widened. There were gasps from the others as he descended into the void. Pip and Tina reached out and grabbed him before he disappeared into the dusty gloom. They wrenched him to safety and the four were together again.

'There – look! Come on the door is open.'

There was no time to talk and they sprinted for the entrance. To their relief, this time, they actually made it outside the perimeter. It was still thick with mist but they weren't going to let that stop them. The four teenagers ploughed on into the grey soup. The ground was vibrating violently, as if consumed by an earthquake. It shook so hard that they all fell. The link between them was broken and each one scrambled to find the other. The sound of falling stone and smashing glass was deafening.

'Help me, someone! I—I can't see anything,' a voice shouted from the fog.

'I'm scared, help—help!' There was so much confusion that no one knew who was shouting. It all came to a peak and stopped abruptly.

The explosions stopped. The noises subsided and quietness prevailed. The grey began to evaporate and, before they knew it, the mist slowly withered away and visibility was restored. The sun filtered through the wisps of fading mist and the warmth of summer returned. They finally could see each other. All four of them were a mess, covered in dirt and their clothes were ripped and tattered. But they didn't care. They were safe. The house was just a heap of rubble.

'Wow, we look a mess,' Pip announced breathlessly.

'Are you surprised?' Tina cut in, but before they could say any more, there was a shout from a distance away that caught their attention.

'Hey, you lot, what do you think you're doing on my land?' the voice rang out. They all turned to see an irate farmer approaching, a sheep dog obediently padding along by his side. 'Are those your bikes in the picnic area? I suggest you go and get them before someone else does.'

'Look, mister,' Zade replied, 'we've just got out of that stupid house,' he ranted pointing at the tumbled down wreck.

The old man looked a bit quizzical at first and then burst into a full belly laugh.

'Are you all on drugs or something? That house has been a ruin for hundreds of years, since it burned down.'

'No, we just esc—' Meadow stopped herself in her tracks and thought for a moment. 'Oh my God, he's right.' She looked at the old building and it did honestly look as though it had been dilapidated for years and years. 'Guys, I think we'd better go.'

They each looked at one another and nodded. The old guy muttered as he left them.

'Kids are crazy these days, drugs and what not. Come on, Missy,' he called to his sheep dog, 'you're dull enough without these characters swayin' yer too,' he said as he hobbled away back in the direction he'd come.

'I'm beginning to think the old man is right,' Pip said, shaking his head.

'Hey, look,' Tina said, excitedly pointing to the heap of rubble. 'Look!'

They did as they were asked and stared. The last wisps of mist were receding, but in the middle of all the rubble and fading fog was a figure, a man waving at them. He was dressed in period costume, and for a moment – just a moment – looked like Lord Epacseon Darke.

'Oh my God,' Meadow said, putting her hand to her mouth.

Then he was gone.

All four of them left the site, relived and confused. This whole adventure wasn't what they'd set out for, but the bond did make them stronger. Pip was a more caring person now, and Meadow felt that. They grasped hands, giving eachother a friendly smile. This made Meadow very happy.

Zade, too, had changed. He wasn't as forceful and realised his way wasn't always the best way. Tina, on the other hand, had toughened up and didn't let anyone push her around after that day.